REAPERS of the DUST

REAPERS of the DUST

A Prairie Chronicle

Lois Phillips Hudson

MINNESOTA HISTORICAL SOCIETY PRESS
St. Paul • 1984

The author wishes to thank the following for permission to reprint material which first appeared in their pages: *The Atlantic, The Reporter, The New Yorker.*

First published 1965 by Little, Brown and Company
Reprint edition 1984 by the Minnesota Historical Society Press
10 9 8 7 6 5 4 3 2 1

MANUFACTURED IN THE UNITED STATES OF AMERICA
INTERNATIONAL STANDARD BOOK NUMBER 0-87351-177-8
Library of Congress Cataloging in Publication Data

Hudson, Lois Phillips, 1927-
Reapers of the dust.

I. Title.
PS3558.U3R4 1984 813′.54 84-14720

FOR
MY MOTHER

Mary Aline Runner
1901–1964

Et lux perpetua luceat eis.

Contents

Preface to the Reprint Edition

WHEN I AM ASKED whether all the stories in this book are "true," I reply that of course they are, even though I know well enough that I am not answering that question in exactly the same spirit in which it was asked. After "The King's Birthday" was first published in the December 24, 1959, *Reporter*, the magazine received a letter that read, in part,

> In my two years or so of reading *The Reporter* regularly, I have read a number of those remarkable semi-autobiographical short stories by Lois Phillips Hudson. . . . Mrs. Hudson appears to be someone about my own age (32) with childhood memories very similar to my own. . . . The people she describes somehow seem to be people I knew myself. Her most recent is a classic indeed. It is billed as a short story, with the implication that it is fiction—but I don't believe it. These people and events are too real. I wonder if Miss Kretchmer read the story, and if so, what her thoughts were. (Probably her name wasn't Miss Kretchmer; that much could be fiction, but no more.)

Twenty-five years after a *Reporter* editor kindly sent a copy of Mr. Wallace B. Riley's letter on to me, it still gives me a little rush of storyteller's elation. The only "fact" he had right was my age! Mr. Riley's response was not naive; it was exactly the response most serious writers of fiction sweat blood for—utter conviction in the reader that "these people and events are too real" to have existed "only in the imagination" of the writer.

But as Byron wrote in *Don Juan,* "truth is always strange; / Stranger than fiction; if it could be told." The writer of fiction explores that daily *unimaginable* reality we all live in, and tries, according to her / his vision of it, to make a work of art that simply renders some segment of it *imaginable.* In *Science and Human Values,* his brilliant plea for that enlargement of our imaginations which alone can save our planet, J. Bronowski says,

> When Coleridge tried to define beauty, he returned always to one deep thought: beauty, he said, is "unity in variety." Science is nothing else than the search to discover unity in the wild variety of nature—or more exactly, in the variety of our experience. Poetry, painting, the arts are the same search, in Coleridge's phrase, for unity in variety.

If the writer is successful, she / he imposes an order on "the wild variety of human experience" which results in a "truth" that is, paradoxically, far more convincing than that unfathomable reality Byron speaks of. Cleanth Brooks and Robert Penn Warren, in "The Intentions of Fiction," have called this truth "the truth of coherence." They do not concern themselves with what percentage of the details in a story may have been plucked from the author's own life; rather, it is what the author *intends* to do with these details that determines a story's genre. History, biography, and journalism must present details that exactly *correspond* to the frequently chaotic world they describe; fiction must concern itself with "the *coherent* relating of action, character, and meaning." They conclude, "There are positive advantages in clearly distinguishing between truth of correspondence and truth of coherence, and fixing upon the latter as the peculiar province of fiction."

After publishing several stories which did draw a large proportion of their events and characters (though perhaps not so many as Mr. Riley supposed) from my own experience, I had learned enough about how to use that experience. When I wrote "The King's Birthday" I was able to stretch my "fictional" wings farther than I had before, and fly a goodly distance into "the peculiar province of fiction." There I was able to explore some very difficult realities in such a way that Mr. Riley would find it the most convincing of all my stories and feel that the people caught in these painful realities were "somehow people I knew myself." His letter made me feel that I had, indeed, arrived in the place where I wanted to be.

The idea for the story occurred to me when the Palo Alto school district, where I was then living, became caught up in the beginnings of that controversy we still are far from resolving: is it appropriate for Christian carols, or even the story of the Nativity, to be used in the public schools at Christmas time? On the one hand, I had total sympathy and respect for the non-Christian families, many of whom had been persecuted in the name of the Baby Jesus; on the other hand, I thought I knew what kind of tenth-rate "stories" and "music" would be cranked out, memorized, and performed by millions of innocent children—Christian and non-Christian. I expected still another inundation of junk, along with the then burgeoning television, sweeping away what I viewed as the infinitely superior (aesthetically speaking) words of the King James Bible and the music of two millennia of western culture. (Some Christmas music goes back, ironically but not surprisingly, to pre-Christian tradition: "Oh Come, Oh Come, Emmanuel" is a ninth-century Latin hymn based on a Hebrew chant. What scrupulously inoffensive little ditty can possibly "replace" it?) This is the kind of dilemma that sends a writer's mind ranging into "the wild varieties of [her own] experience." I thought of my childhood Christmases in both church and school, and I thought of my Jewish friends.

When I was in graduate school in Ithaca, New York, I became acquainted with a brilliant Jewish woman, somewhat older than I, who had been graduated from Barnard in 1933, hoping to teach in public school. There were no jobs in the city, and she was beginning to hunt farther and farther into the hinterlands when she was awarded a scholarship to do graduate work in Germany. (She often remarked, "What a year for *me* to go to Germany!") Imagining Lillian going not to Germany, but to Cleveland, North Dakota, was all the start I needed.

I wrote the story about the problem that may never be solved to everyone's satisfaction, and about another problem I had had with the metaphor of "the melting pot" since I first encountered it (in school, of course) at the age of nine or ten, and conjured for myself a terrifying image of tiny people of all shapes and colors disappearing into a bubbling cauldron. My childish instincts had told me that Nature loved variety long before my culture had got around to a superficial embracing of it in the mid-1960s, and I grieved (and still grieve) over our inability to achieve true equality while preserving all our splendid uniquenesses—in short, to find unity in variety.

In the narrower sense of the "truth of correspondence," the only "true" aspects of the story are the setting—the home of my beloved Great-aunt Elva and the little church which still stands across the street from where her house used to be. My friend Lillian did read the story, "identified" with Miss Kretchmer as any reader must in order to be involved in it at all, and never once suspected that she was the inspiration for the young teacher who got her name from the wheat-germ box in my cupboard. And no matter how convincing was "the truth of coherence" in my story, in "real life" no such Christmas program could possibly have happened in that church at that time.

Perhaps the most satisfying tribute to the "truth" in my story was the response of its first reader. Before I sent my manuscripts anywhere else, I always submitted them to my mother, who was my most valuable critic. (How I miss her!) Even she was fooled. She wrote that she found no inaccuracies in the story, and then mused, "I never realized you were in school the year we had that little red-headed teacher from New York." My teacher was a North Dakota native and I have no memories of any instructors, Jewish or red-headed, from New York.

Every day we encounter events we would not believe if they were presented to us as fiction, because every day millions of absolutely incredible things really do happen. Our inability to imagine other lives (and we surely cannot love until we can imagine) has been a major factor in our ability to obliterate those lives. How many of us have really imagined the Holocaust that was beginning when my friend went to Germany to study mathematics? Indeed, it is a truth so incredible that an incredibly sinister group of neo-Nazis is, incredibly, succeeding in persuading some of us that it never happened. In November, 1945, Bronowski visited Nagasaki, where he "met the experience of mankind. . . . Each of us in his own way learned that his imagination had been dwarfed." He goes on:

> The gravest indictment of our *generalized culture* is, in fact, that it erodes our sense of the context in which judgments must be made. . . . When I returned from the physical shock of Nagasaki, I tried to persuade my colleagues in governments and in the United Nations that Nagasaki should be preserved exactly as it was then. I wanted all future conferences on disarmament, and on other issues which weigh the fates of nations, to be held in that ashy, clinical sea of rubble. . . . Alas, my official colleagues thought nothing of my scheme; on the contrary, they pointed out to me that delegates would be uncomfortable in Nagasaki. (My italics.)

I believe, along with Bronowski, that the artist's major job is to help us to imagine the unimaginable, to reveal to us the dark anguish in individual human hearts which enables us, acting collectively, to do incredible things. It is not the artist's job to *solve* problems—*all* of us must work together on solutions—but it *is* the artist's job to help us examine them. Thus I was pleased by another generous letter from a psychologist in Michigan who wrote, of "Gopher Hunting," that he had done his internship in the state mental hospital in Jamestown where "we saw a phenomenon we called the 'farm wife's syndrome.' . . . Your last story very effectively explains some of the things I have been wondering about." (I'm not going to tell, here, how much of "Gopher Hunting" is "true"!) Then Dr. Karl Menninger asked me for permission to duplicate the story for use in his Kansas clinic. He felt that it would help his staff, particularly the men, become more sensitive to the lives of their women patients.

It seems that no matter how many "facts" we can discover, it is still art, as Lionel Trilling said, which "records the most important judgments we possess as to the value of experience." I doubt that we can *remember* things we have not at least partially *imagined,* and I wonder if an insufficient body of great writing about the Holocaust constitutes one of the reasons why it seems so remote from the consciousness of most of us.

A much more recent example is that of Jonestown, Guyana. To my knowledge, no one has yet written a book that has come close to creating that "truth of coherence" which will reach our imaginations and root the causes of Jonestown in our memories. No one has yet given us a mother standing in that line of over nine hundred people—a mother who has left friends and family and gone to a frighteningly distant and strange land, labored inhumanly to clear the jungle and grow food, all to give her baby a better life than she could foresee for that baby here—a mother standing in a line falling before her into individual human beings dying their individual deaths in agonized retching convulsions, looking down into the face of the baby who is not going to have any life at all and giving it the drink of Kool-Aid laced with cyanide. Although it happened only six years ago, I have many students, even some graduate students, who recognize no significance in the words "Jonestown, Guyana." How incredible! If we do not manage to *imagine* the realities we live in, as Bronowski and Jonathan Schell and Helen Caldicott have told us, how can we possibly deal with them?

"Only connect," E. M. Forster advised writers of fiction; help your readers (and yourself, of course), to see how actions, characters, and meanings relate to each other in a comprehensible vision of the human condition. I hope these offerings from "the peculiar province of fiction" can help us remember the lives of people struggling through the Great Depression, and, far beyond that one time and one place, help us imagine the lives of people in any time and any place who, like me, struggle to find sense and beauty in "the wild variety of human experience."

Lois Phillips Hudson

❧❧❧❧ The Dust Storm

TWO SPRINGS AGO, according to local newspapers and to coughing, red-eyed service-station operators in the Rocky Mountains, we drove through the worst dust storm Wyoming had suffered in eighteen years. The wind was prematurely aging the young Rockies, pushing dusty fingers under the loosening fragments of thin topsoil that covered the grazing plateaus, picking up the small greenish gravel from the road shoulders, and hurling dust and gravel into the air at sixty miles an hour. If we dipped into a trough between plateaus, its shelter enabled us to see the laden wind rising over the mountains and the sky running in massive dirty currents above us. After reaching the Coast we replaced the badly pitted window glass, had the car repainted, and cleaned the seats, floor mats, and window crevices. Yet months after we thought we had breathed the last Wyoming grit, we turned on the defroster and blew bits of the Rocky Mountains all through the car.

Dust storms are like that: no matter how many times you clean or how much you scrub and repaint and dig into crevices, you are always finding another niche the dust has found. And in the dust is the smell of mortality, of fertility swept away and spring vanished.

For me the storm was the revival of the nightmares of childhood, and I breathed again the dust of the storms that drove my family from our North Dakota farm. I remember particularly the storm of the spring when I was in the second grade. That morning in late March the sky had the kind of height that only the sky of a prairie or a desert or a sea can have; it makes its own boundaries, its symmetry never spiked by the reaching of tall trees, never crowded by the peaks of mountains. It was the kind of blue that can come only from the cleansing of melted snow.

But now, after the earth had softened for a few days and allowed the great banks of snow to sink into her embrace, seemingly chilled by her own compliance, she had hardened again. For a week now, the plowed furrows had been so full of frost that we could walk them as if they were railroad tracks. Gone were the rivulets bearing the snowbanks out into the fields where the fetal leaves sprang forth, marvelously green in the rich black mud. This usually happened, of course; you could expect an early thaw to be followed by a hard freeze. Even so, those first days of fast melting, with their joyous profusion of water, were enough to instill in the most drought-embittered farmer the resolution to try one more crop before he got out.

The ambition nourished by that first thawing sent the farmers out to get in a few days of early plowing, to burn away the thistles collected against the fences, to oil machinery that may have sat under six feet of snow all winter, or just to tramp over their land to check the depth of the moisture and to visualize the August fields. On this morning my father planned to mend fences, and as he piled his heavy ancient equipment into the rear seat of our 1929 Ford he sang one of his favorite songs, "The Bulldog on the Bank and the Bullfrog in the Pool." He was singing because perhaps this year there would be no drought, and perhaps our share-the-crop landlord, who ran a clothing store twenty miles away, would let him plant the way he wanted to plant — not insisting on having the entire crop be soil-depleting wheat — and perhaps the prices would go up enough next fall so that he could buy a secondhand tractor and retire our worn-out team. It was not often that he sang, and I felt good hearing him, because I thought the three-mile ride to school would not be as silent and austere as it usually was.

My mother pushed me out the door after one last "No" to my whinings about taking off my winter underwear. As soon as I felt the wind, I had to admit to myself that I was glad I had lost the argument. This argument was mostly a ritual anyway, to demonstrate my confidence in spring.

On this day, even though I knew the wind meant another month in long underwear, I was happy, because a really hard wind was a wondrous playmate. My mother had shown me how to raise my coat at arm's length over my head and, holding the two corners of it, let the wind fill it and send me sailing along like an iceboat. She had often told me of iceboating on Lake Michigan when she taught school there in the years before the depression, and for some reason the only clear ideas I had about how life would be "when good times come again" were all tied up with iceboating. Except for that, the idea of "good times" was very dim to me, despite my parents' efforts to explain it in material terms: oranges every day, new coats instead of garments pieced together from the least worn parts of discarded adults' coats, a car that was maybe only about two or three years old, for the advent of streamlining had humiliatingly outdated our square old Model A. The thought of being able to visit our relatives in Michigan and go iceboating was the clearest conception I had of good times; surely this was the sort of exhilaration we would all feel every day when good times came again.

There was a good chance that the wind might provide some real excitement that day, it seemed to me. As we drove through the stubble fields of our farm, a miniature whirlwind twisted up from the dry ruts of the road, spun toward us, and broke itself against the car in a small fury of powdered earth, pebbles and straw. My father sneezed and jerked the car around a rock in the road.

"Do you think there will be a hard wind today?" I asked, trying not to sound too eager and to make dignified conversation about the weather the way grownups did and thus sound interesting to my father. (He always told me not to talk unless I could say something interesting, but I could never figure out just which of my ideas were interesting.)

"*You'd* be happy if it blew ninety miles an hour, wouldn't you?" was his only answer. His light mood was gone already and we weren't even on the main road yet. I was quiet the rest of the way to school.

In school I stared out over the heads of the first-graders from my desk in the middle row of the three-grade room and watched the wind. I could see the Koslovs' washing hung in their back yard. Trouser legs bestrode the air, and Old Man Koslov's big-bellied underwear bent double-jointed knees and elbows in drunken imitation of its hard-drinking owner. I looked at Ivan Koslov to see if he was aware that the whole primary room was grinning over his grandfather's underwear, but he was lost in a discouraged slump over his reading book. My father had told me that all the Russians ("Roosians," he called them) were dumb, because they plowed up the land in the fall so the wind could blow it over everybody else's land all through the winter and spring, and they didn't know how to farm to keep the fertility in the soil, and, worst of all, they wouldn't even bother to learn the English language. This last I knew was true; the parents of many of my Russian schoolmates still didn't speak English even though they had lived in North Dakota for many years. It never occurred to me at the time that Ivan and the others might have some excuse for their difficulty with reading. All I knew was that reading class was pretty boring and that it was a relief when the recess bell rang.

At recess, when there wasn't too much snow, we used to play a game called anty-eye-over, using the roof of a long low appendage to the main building. In this game the players on one side throw the ball over to their opponents, yelling "Anty-eye-over!" as a signal that it is coming. If the receivers catch the ball, they try to surprise the other team by sneaking around the building and capturing players by hitting them with the ball. The teams took up their positions on either side of a narrow shed covering two separate hallways that led to the two separate little rooms with their four bitterly cold board seats over the trench below, into which the janitor dumped enough lye to half suffocate the users of the rooms. Most of the length of the shed was for the obvious purpose of removing the toilets as far as possible from the classrooms, and so it provided a generous space for our game. On this day, though, the wind did such ridiculous things with the ball that we had to give up and play the wind's games. We used our coats for sails or experimented with nonchalant off-balance poses leaning into the wind.

In the Koslovs' field behind the school, last year's dead tumbleweeds (we called them Russian thistles) unwound their roots from the disintegrating earth and came sweeping erratically across the ground at us. We played a tense game of tag with these brown stinging monsters, the tangible claws of the unseen wind, the articulation of its anger. They would hook into each other and roll in a dragging bumping wave till they caught in a fence.

By noon the whirlwinds were everywhere and had dried up the surface of the fields. The whirlwinds rushed across the playground sucking up lunch bags, old papers, and caps of children trying to eat their lunches outside. I was fast losing my enthusiasm for this wind. Only last summer a big tornado had passed less than ten miles south of us. We had all gone down into the storm cellar to wait for it to come and pull our house up into its widening funnel. It had spared us, but the cloudburst that went with it had not. Yet the things the tornado did to other people made us ashamed to complain about the ruin we suffered from the cloudburst.

I was through with this wind as a playmate. The sky was already dim with dust and the dirt was splatting into my eyes and mouth. I went back into the schoolroom and watched Ivan Koslov and his sister Neva and some of the others eating apples. They all got boxes of apples from the relief. "Why don't *you* go on relief?" they asked me. I didn't answer them. My mother had told me we were too proud to be on relief. My father had gone to apply for a WPA job on the highway once, but the administrator had asked him to say that we were even poorer than we were, and he wouldn't lie. He knew most of the others had lied to get their jobs, but he would have starved rather than resort to a "Roosian trick." So I was really proud that we didn't have apples.

I turned away from the feast and got a book to read. It was a book of fairy tales, and in the corner of a map on the end-papers was a supposedly whimsical depiction of the North Wind. He had a fat dissipated face with billowy cheeks, and his eyes glittered greedily under the icicled eyebrows. By the time lunch hour was over the sounds of the god's hunger and of his reverberating digestion were too much for the teacher to talk above, and she let all three grades have an unprecedent-ed extra art period. But even the luxury of cutting colored paper and making clay animals did not relieve our tension. We feared daytime darkness as savages do, knowing that the earth's disasters were our own.

By four o'clock, dismissal time, there was a besieged line of vehicles outside the school gates. Most of the men were in open wagons, as was my father, because very few people could afford buggies, and practically all of the cars in that area were, like ours, too vulnerable to trust to such weather.

Some of the men were standing on the lee side of their horses, like Arabs in a sandstorm — but not my father. He wouldn't ask a horse to take anything he wouldn't take. He sat on the plank thrown across the sides of the wagon box, the bill of his earmuffed hunting cap slanting over his eyes and the collar of his sheepskin coat hunched up along the back of his neck. He had done what he could for the horses; there were old blankets over their backs under the harness and feed bags up over their nostrils for dust filters.

Before I had got a foot on the hub of the wheel, which I used as a step, my father reached down his gloved hand and jerked me up into the wagon. Although we usually sat apart — I often in the back hanging my legs over the flapping tail-gate — this time he pulled me hard against him to give me all the protection he could. He wrapped a heavy cowhide around me, draping its tannery-smelling stiffness over my head, with the dusty tickling hairs touching my cheek. Each vehicle in turn detached itself from the group, leaving the illusion of solidarity for the reality of solitude in the shrieking storm. The three miles home took us almost two hours.

Usually on my return from school my mother would welcome me with some casual questions about what I had done that day. But now she kept her face turned away from me and greeted me with an order to wash and pour some milk. I went to the small wooden box under the windowsill where we kept the Mason jars full of whole milk we saved out before running the rest of the milking through the cream separator. We kept the box there because so much cold air came in around the window in winter.

As I bent to pick up the milk I noticed the damp rags that were stuffed into the cracks between the window frame and the sash and along the sills. They were black with dust.

"Boy, there's a lot of dirt here!" I said.

My mother didn't look up from the stove. "That's not the only place there's a lot of dirt." Only twice before had her voice sounded like that — once when my grandfather died and once when I accidentally broke the only window in our dark little kitchen. Terrified, I stared about me and saw that the dust was sifting down everywhere.

The kitchen was actually a lean-to addition to the other two rooms in the house, and keeping it livable was a losing battle but one that my parents never gave up. Once a year in the spring, before outdoor work began, and when no more melting snow could seep down from the roof and stain the walls, we spent the money for paint. It was the cheapest calcimine available, but things did look much better for a while, and the annual refurbishing of the kitchen was a kind of treat for us.

Inspired by the thaw, we had painted just after the last snow stain had dried in the plaster. Along with the farmers who had planted too early, we had been too ambitious, too eager for spring. Now this house that my mother was always so ashamed of would bear the depressing murkiness of the storm all year long. There would be summer days when the thermometer read one hundred degrees outside, and yet she would have to build a fire in the coal stove to heat the water for washing and heating the sadirons. There would be the months of dim winter when the sun rose long cold hours after we did and set again in a frozen peach-colored sky hours before suppertime. And through all those days she would look up from her iron or her washboard or her kneading or her nightly mending by the kerosene lamp to behold those foul darkening streaks on the walls that contained all of her life — all of it that was not spent outside toiling in whatever black earth remained to us.

In that same awful voice she broke out, "Oh, what's the use of trying!"

If she was going to cry, then here indeed was the end of hope — things could only get worse, always and always worse.

The next morning the sky was very blue again, in the way it has of being especially blue just after storms. My father had gone looking for the stock. The dust, catching in the Russian thistles that were clinging to the fences, had packed so hard and piled so high in several sheltered areas that the cattle and horses had walked right up the dirt banks and over the fence.

Once, in the memory of my own grandparents, that atomized earth had been nearly impossible to break with a plow. Enriched by the floods of vanished rivers, the droppings and bones of numberless generations of buffalo, the mulch of thousands of summers of grass, it waited now, an unsalvageable encumbrance upon the sagging fence — waited to be carried farther and farther, scalding other fields in its passing, finally coming to its grave in the Mississippi Delta. There was no rain to hold it for us, no rain to nourish clutching roots before the next wind.

A prairie child, walking in the loneliness of great spaces, absorbs familiarity with eternity. In that enduring loneliness I might have existed through centuries of freedom and bounty, when the grass rose to the shoulders of the buffalo and the grass and the buffalo fed each other, and the land and the grass held each other against wind and drought. This eternity of abundance had spread a feast for the bread-hungry world and for the soul of the farmer — but the farmer's soul had been too small to cherish the immense heritage.

Through the storm I was being informed that this eternity could not survive the ignorance of men. I was learning why my father sorrowed for the land, angrily grinding the dust in his teeth and thinking of the impossible combination of men and elements he faced — the illiterate "Roosians," the exploiting farmers, their exploiting absentee landlords, the wind, the drought. No dust storms began on his farm, but once the wind was full of dust his farm suffered along with the rest.

While I was eating my oatmeal the morning after the storm,

my mother said, "Oh, I just feel so sorry for Daddy. He worked all morning in that wind yesterday on the north fence." This was all she said about the storm.

My father came in to take me to school. He didn't even say whether he had managed to round up the stock. A wind too big to allow communication was still all around us and inside of us.

Gopher Hunting

IT IS WHERE there are the fewest distinctions between men and women that there can be the most bitterness between them. If a woman's major function in life is to contribute additional muscles and energy to her husband's physical battle for survival, then her usefulness will be judged by the same criteria that determine the usefulness of males. Such habits of thinking result in constant comparisons, usually to the disadvantage of females, so that women are seldom allotted any niche to dominate.

Even in the kitchen of a North Dakota home less than a generation ago, men had the feeling that women must be somehow inferior. There, the average farm wife, like my mother, still baked her own bread, churned her own butter, rendered out the lard for the crust of her pies, cultivated and harvested the family's vegetables, and nurtured, then executed, the chickens fried for the Sunday table. But still, as my father would often observe, "It's just *practice*. I can cook better than *any* woman if I put my mind to it. Of course, there may be some things a woman is born to be better at. Like bathing a baby, for instance. But I reckon I could even do a pretty fair job at that, too, if I ever had to."

North Dakota men didn't bathe babies, so the question never came up. On the other hand, the question of women and the important tasks of life came up all the time, and since women were judged by how much wheat they could shock or how many cows they could milk, they were almost always doomed to inferiority. Once in a great while a woman made a good showing, and my father would sound honestly admiring when he said something like, "You ought to have seen Hilda Jensen out there helping Aaron dehorn those calves. Why, she's as tough as a man! Quite a gal!"

When beauty and graciousness appear in such an existence, they are irrelevant, and they perish like any other delicate untended thing. Beauty fades into a dusty sun squint, and graciousness dies in exhaustion.

As a small girl on a North Dakota farm some thirty years ago, I probably resented the fate that made me female no more than did most of my contemporaries. There seemed to be nothing for us to look forward to except spending our lives as poor seconds to men. We could learn to live with that prospect or we could smolder hopelessly. Some of my friends achieved a resentful peace — that is, they openly, if grudgingly, admitted boys were superior. Some of them, like me, smoldered and fought. Our obsession with our inferiority we kept secret, and we courted opportunities to demonstrate our superiority. The boys, amused by our fanaticism, patronized and mocked us with ridiculous dares, not one of which we failed to accept. I remember the time when one of my second-grade classmates dared me to shinny up the iron pole that supported the top landing of the fire escape on the schoolhouse. I went all the way, of course, two and a half stories above the cement sidewalk.

But the efforts I made to impress the boys I went to school with were nothing compared to the efforts I made to impress my father. By the time I was seven years old, I was driving a team of horses up and down a hayfield while he worked in the back of the hayrack, pitching the hay forward to make room for more, piling it on the revolving teeth of the hayloader. When we transferred the load to the loft or the haystack, I tramped it down as he forked it up to me. As I floundered back and forth, sidestepping the flashing tines of the hayfork, reeling from the heat, choking in the swarming dust and chaff, lifting my dead legs over and over again with the false energy of my mania, I would tell myself that no boy could keep up with a man who pitched hay as fast as my father.

I fed calves, herded cattle, weeded the garden, husked corn, and hauled buckets of water up the long hill to the house, always wondering what more a boy could do to please my father. In winter when he hunted jack rabbits over miles of snow-covered prairie, I plodded after him, keeping my tracks straight like an Indian's and trying to stretch my stride as long as his.

"I swan, that child walks exactly like her father," my grandmother would say disapprovingly. Her tone didn't bother me at all; I was proud of what she had said.

But there was one thing all boys could do that I couldn't. I couldn't kill a gopher — or any other living thing, for that matter. This I knew was the failing that betrayed all my other efforts to become as useful and as admirable as a boy. My cousin, who was four years older than I, earned nearly fifteen dollars a summer by trapping gophers. Two cents a tail could add up remarkably, especially if you cut the big tails in half. My father would keep pointing out that if I were only like Warren I could earn some money too. Finally, the summer that I was going on eight, I decided that I would simply have to start trapping gophers. My father was very pleased. He located a gopher hole behind the chickenhouse and said, "Now here's some easy money right here. I'll fetch you a trap and you'll have him in an hour or so."

As we approached the hole I felt sicker and sicker, and the sicker I got the more I hated myself for being female. He showed me how to set the trap, but he wouldn't put it in the hole. He wanted me to think that I was earning this money myself. I pried the serrated jaws apart and laid the trap in the freshly dug earth. Then I took a big rock and pounded the stake on the trap chain deep into the ground, so that if the teeth caught the gopher's foot he couldn't drag the whole thing away before I got there to finish him off.

My father went whistling off to the fields and I slunk into the grove and sat in my swing. But I didn't swing, because I felt that somebody who was doing what I was doing ought not to be playing. I tried to imagine taking a rock in my hand and bringing it down on the head of a tiny frantic animal whose foot bled around a trap. I wanted to pray that God would make him stick his head squarely into the death I had set out for him, but that crunching snap was not the sort of thing one could pray for. Besides, every night I prayed that God would turn me into a boy while I slept, and I thought that if He was anything like parents, I was more likely to get one big favor from Him if I was careful not to ask for too many little ones.

I have no idea how long I sat in the swing before sneaking back around the chickenhouse to the trap; perhaps, measured by the clock (of all inventions the most irrelevant to human misery), it was no more than five minutes. The brainless levity of the hens and roosters in the chicken yard revolted me. It did not matter to them that a charming creature from the fields had to die for stealing a bit of the corn we showered upon them in return for a few eggs. I picked up the big rock I had pounded the stake with, to prove to myself that I could use it if I had to.

The trap was empty. I stood over it a moment until I realized that the gopher might come up and be caught before my eyes. I rushed back to the swing and began all over again the wretched process of hardening myself. After another five minutes I visited the trap again, and once more retreated, trembling with relief.

I made two or three more trips before I broke. Once I had made my resolution, I leaped from the swing, distraught at the possibility of being too late. The trap was still empty. I flung a stone on the trigger and jumped when it sprang shut. Then I wrenched the stake out of the ground and dragged the trap back to the barn, where I hung it on its peg. It clanked against the wall a couple of times, calling "Coward" after me.

Had I been craftier, I would have sprung the trap and allowed my father to think that a twig had fallen into it, or that the gopher had managed to spring it without being caught, as they sometimes did. That would have shown that I had done my best but that the gopher was too smart for me and knew how to hang on to his two-cent tail. But I was not crafty, and I spent the rest of the morning steeling myself against the pain of my father's disgust.

He was angry as well as disgusted. Gophers were one of the main irritations of his life. They robbed the fields and riddled the pastures with holes so that horses and cows would stumble into them and break their legs. Not only had I once again demonstrated my foolish weakness, I had also betrayed him. He stamped out to the chickenhouse and set the trap himself. The next morning he came in from milking and said, "Well, I got your gopher for you. If you want the tail, go get it. Otherwise, throw him out in the pasture somewheres, so he don't stink up the yard."

I wouldn't have dreamed of taking the tail in for that two cents; I knew the sneer that would sit on my father's face all the way to town. Not that I didn't want the two cents, which was more money than I might see in two or three weeks. I stopped thinking about how much candy the two pennies would buy when I saw the dead gopher, his disheveled head bleeding and his pert little jaws askew, with the curved white teeth pointing out at chaotic angles. I picked him up tenderly by his valuable tail and walked out to the pasture. There I took a stick and scooped a grave for him, covering it with blades of grass and the indifferent faces of dandelions.

Neither my father nor I had forgotten my failure on the day Peter Liljeqvist, one of the town boys, walked out to our farm to ask my father if he could spend a few hours trapping gophers on our property. He was a year older than I, and from the dark tan of his staunch face to the lithe vigor of his slim legs, he was compellingly masculine. I could see that my father longed for a son like him, but though I resented him for being a boy, still I felt an unwilling attraction to him. As boys went, he was one of the nicer ones in school. Perhaps he had some sort of special feeling for me, too, for it occurs to me now that he surely didn't need to go three miles from town to find more gophers than he could catch in six months.

It was routine, in a male-dominated world, for him to nod toward me and ask my father, "O.K. if she goes along?"

My father hooted. "Sure, she can go along. Sure. Big help she'll be to you."

My mother interrupted him. "Just a minute and I'll pack you a lunch," she said.

"Nice stand of wheat you got out there along the road," Peter remarked easily but respectfully to my father. Good man talk. It would have done me no good at all to say the same thing.

My mother came to the door with the lunch in a gallon pail. The last thing my father said was, "Can't count on her for any help, Pete. You know what girls are like."

With a chivalry that nearly quenched my jealousy of him, Peter said, "Oh, she can carry the lunch. That's enough help."

We headed for the pasture, walking into the sun, with our shadows diverging at a squat angle to the left behind us. Peter's only equipment was a long cord, one end of which he made into a noose, and a knife for cutting off tails. When we came to what looked like a recently made hole, he arranged the noose around the mouth of it. Then he tested the breeze with a wet finger and we moved downwind. He knelt and sat back on his heels, clutching the end of the cord, prepared to yank it up tight the instant a head emerged.

My stomach felt the same way it had that day in the swing, but I was determined to prove to Peter that I could be as quiet and purposeful as any male. For a while we sat absorbed in anticipation – he in eagerness, I in dread. But Peter was not a very patient hunter, or perhaps he preferred exploring to hunting. He never wanted to stay at one place very long, and we wandered farther and farther, pausing to sit by a burrow now and then as much for rest as for trapping. We were having an argument about which holidays were the best – Christmas, birthdays, the Fourth of July, or Halloween – when a small striped head darted up through Peter's noose and startled us both. Before he could jerk the noose, the gopher was nearly out of the hole and he caught only its hind legs. It flopped on its back, twisted up its head, and raked Peter's fist with its long front teeth. "Ow!" he yelled, and in his shock he smashed down the rock he held in his other hand. It was a mangling blow to the gopher's little belly, but it did not die. It lay writhing at our feet.

"Go get a bigger rock!" Peter screamed.

Even if he had dared let go of the string, he couldn't have moved. I knew that we had to end the gopher's agony, but I also knew that I could never do it. I found a rock I could barely lift and lugged it back to Peter. He dropped it on the gopher's head, and the legs in the noose kicked once and were still.

We stood there for a minute and then Peter said, "Let's eat our lunch." The vacancy in my stomach was not caused by hunger, but I agreed. We moved a few yards away, turned our backs on the gopher, and opened the pail. "Boy, homemade bread!" Peter exclaimed. "My mother hardly ever makes it."

"Mine always does," I said. "My father doesn't like store bread. But I do," I added. It always seemed to me that store bread was much more aristocratic than homemade, but it made me happy to have Peter think the large thick slices with their heavy crusts were a treat. I was so cheered by his enthusiasm that I found the dry sandwiches going down with unwonted smoothness. We finished off our bottle of water and stuck it back in the pail. Our dread of the gopher was gone. I felt terribly sorry for him but I wasn't afraid to look at him any more. After all, I wasn't the guilty one; it was all Peter's doing. Peter drew his knife from his pocket with his old aplomb, snapped out the blade, and severed the bushy little tail. The great red ants had arrived and were at their task. He brushed them away and freed his noose.

We had no luck with the holes we tried after that, but our ramblings between burrows netted us a hoard of the natural litter that children feel compelled to save and store away — three discarded snakeskins, an abandoned bird's nest, the empty blue shell of a robin's egg, inexplicably far from the nearest trees, the thin, loose-toothed skull of a rabbit, and a delicate forest of toadstools pushing up from a dried heap of cow dung. We were skirting the edge of a wide slough a mile or so from our farm when we noticed a hawk circling persistently right over us. With his eyes on the hawk, Peter stumbled over the moist mound at the edge of a new gopher hole and we both remembered that we were supposed to be collecting tails.

"Hey, I bet the old hawk is just up there waiting for this gopher to come out. I bet he saw him go in this hole," Peter said, and his reasoning seemed to be corroborated as the hawk's shadow swept viciously over the mound at our feet. "Let's drown him out!" Peter cried. He found a rock and settled his noose in place while I poured the water down the hole. After the fourth of fifth pailful I ceased to worry about the little creature down there shuddering in the dark while an erratic flood gushed in upon him. I was sure he wasn't there. It seemed to me that the other end of the tunnel must empty back into the slough.

I began to regard the circulation of water, a gallon at a time, as a useful activity in itself, and I was not at all prepared when my pail of water erupted in a muddy backwash that boiled out of the hole over my feet and foamed about the sleek dripping head of a half-dead gopher.

At the sight of the flashing tin pail above him, the gopher dived back into his instinctive refuge, but he came clawing out again. Peter yanked his noose, but it had floated harmlessly to one side of the hole, and the gopher hauled himself weakly onto the sloppy ground.

Once again the sudden materializing of our long-sought quarry transfixed us, and we watched stupidly while the gopher's heaving sides pumped air into his collapsing lungs. Finally Peter snatched up his rock and dropped it. It slammed into the mud splattering us both up to our waists, and missing the gopher entirely. He made a wild plunge between our legs and disappeared into an old burrow just behind us.

"Phooey!" Peter spat. "Let him go! I hope that old hawk gets him the first time he comes out!"

He looked at our muddy legs. "Let's go down to the slough and wash," he said.

We took off our shoes and started sloshing the murky water up our shins. "I hear a frog!" Peter said. "Let's catch him."

"Aw, you can't tell where a frog is by the sound he makes," I said. I ought to have known; I had squandered hours leaping after a wily croak that switched direction while I was still in mid-air.

"I bet I can," he said, and he made a spectacular jump to the nearest hummock sticking out of the water. He wavered a little and dug his toes into the mud and said, "See, he was right here, just like I said. He just jumped into the water when he seen me coming."

It seemed to me that if the frogs were going to jump every time we jumped, our chances of catching one were pretty slim, but I didn't want Peter to think he was the only one who could make it from the shore to that hummock, so I said, "Get out of the way. Here I come." He stepped to the next hummock and I took a little run and landed squarely in his oozing footprints.

"Jeez, I didn't think you could do it," he said.

"I can do a six-foot standing broad jump," I said. "My father took me out and measured it one day. He said if I was only a boy he could make a champion out of me."

Peter was distant and crestfallen. "I bet I can make it to that one over there," he said.

"I bet *I* can *too*," I said.

He gave himself a shove and lit with one bare heel slanting back into the slough. Then he stepped over on a teetering rock and slapped it back and forth against the water, trying to heckle me into missing my mark. But I didn't miss it. We jumped about for a while, daring each other, and then we began looking for frogs again.

The slough was probably not more than two feet deep at its center, but it covered a couple of acres or so, and my mother had warned me to stay away from it. Even if the water wasn't dangerously deep, there was a chance of getting stuck in the mud and drowning. Tall spiky reeds cast shadows so dark that the slough appeared to be bottomless, and frothy blotches of gleaming slime ringed the shores of our little hummocks like a green disease, while long ribbons of the stuff trailed through the water.

It was a place best suited for frogs, blackbirds, and mosquitoes, and the more clearly we saw that nothing human could prevail over such a wilderness, the more determined we became to make that wilderness yield us a trophy. Each of us must have known that the hunt was utterly hopeless. Yet we went on, leaping farther and farther into the tangle of weeds and scum, bruising our feet on hidden rocks and scratching our legs and arms against the stiff blades of the reeds. The more guilty I felt for disobeying my mother, the more I believed that capturing a frog would justify me. The more foolish our quest became, the more necessary it was to go on with it.

Hordes of red-winged blackbirds began settling in the rushes around us, and when we hopped too near a tribe of them, they would whir away before us, bold and angry. For every frog we sent splashing into the water, at least five frogs added their ventriloquy to the mounting bedlam. Mosquitoes fastened themselves on us in such exuberant numbers that the only ones we tried to brush away were those feeding upon our mouths and eyelids. And then, before it had even occurred to us to consider such remote and ordinary things as the revolving of the sun, night fell upon us and our madness.

We looked at each other in the dusk and then we looked for the shore we had left so far behind, but all we could see was the thicket of reeds around us.

The birds had gone to roost and the only sound they made was a startling rush of wings into the twilight whenever we came near their roosting places. The frogs became hideously loud; night had given them triumphant and undisputed possession of the slough. The eyes of snakes and hawks slept, and the eyes of the floundering human invaders were blurred and harmless. As soon as a hunter becomes harmless, he feels vulnerable to harm. It is part of the hunting instinct to believe that the savage balance is always maintained; those who do not hunt are hunted. And so as the din of our erstwhile quarry buffeted and surrounded us, we began to have an apprehension of retribution. The noise shaped itself into an invisible menace.

I became aware that the mud around my feet was cold. Peter must have had the same sensation, for he remembered our shoes. Our shoes! How would we ever find them? How would we ever even get back to them?

Prairie children usually have an almost infallible sense of direction, but panic and darkness confused us. Everything looked the same – as hopeless one way as another. We hopped aimlessly to two or three more hummocks. The darkness began to interfere with our accuracy. I mistook the green stuff lapping against a hummock for the solid earth itself and slid to my knees in muck.

The reluctance of that slimy mouth to give back my leg forced a female scream from me, and in that instant I became female. All day long the only thing my sex had meant was that I was inferior, but then in a flash of desperate insight I understood, for the first time in my life, the advantages that logically accrued to females if males were to deny them equality. If boys were smarter, bolder, stronger, and steadier than girls, then Peter was responsible for getting us into this mess and he was supposed to be able to get us out. It was his fault that I had not minded my mother. For once the world was all on my side.

"I don't know which way to go, Peter," I said. "Do you think we'll have to stay here all night?"

I would never have imagined that a show of female weakness could have such an effect on a male. In the society I knew, women never *showed* weakness.

"Of course not!" he declared stoutly. "Come on, let's go this way. You just jump right behind me." All right, I thought, if he gets us lost it'll just be up to him to get us found again. I felt that with him responsible I couldn't get too cold, too hungry, too tired, or too scared. It was the reward of his birthright to suffer for both of us.

And that night his reward was unenviable. *He* was the one who fell in when he thought the slime or a slippery rock was a safe hummock. Profiting by his mistakes, I managed to avoid immersing myself in green scum. Having surrendered myself to femininity, I shrieked each time he fell, but he always struggled up again, cursing in a brave masculine way, and assuring me through mouthfuls of stagnant mud that we were going to be all right.

When we finally could see the shoreline, he grabbed my hand and we ran through the last few feet of water, heedless of hummocks, reeds, or slime.

"You go that way and I'll go this way," he ordered.

We started around the banks of the slough, looking for our shoes. In a few minutes I caught the dull gleam of our lunch pail, and there, unbelievably, were the shoes. By that time we had our bearings and we headed for home, running barefoot over the dewy grass because our feet were too dirty to put back into our shoes.

About a quarter of a mile from home I began to hear my father's voice echoing over the prairie, and I could tell by its direction and rhythm that he was somewhere near the house, berating my mother about something. As we came through the barnyard I heard him say, "Oh, that kid is just an irresponsible nitwit—just another town nitwit. He's probably got them lost ten miles from here." He stopped and I saw the light of a lantern flare up. "I'll hang this out in the south grove and then I'll go get Liljeqvist and round up some men."

"Here we are!" I yelled.

My parents ran toward us. "Where the Sam Hill have you been?" my father shouted furiously. "I ought to lick you with the razor strop."

But he couldn't lick me because he would have had to lick Peter, too, and he didn't dare do that.

My mother made Peter come in the house, filthy as he was, and gave him an old towel to wipe his face and arms with. Then she fed us, while my father sat fuming behind an outdated *Country Gentleman*.

We put an old blanket on the car seat so Peter wouldn't get slime all over it, and he climbed in meekly beside my father. He looked much smaller than when I was following him out of the slough, but still I could never forget that he was the one who had taken the responsibility.

I felt sorry for him, having to sit so small and dirty and sheepish in the scorching heat of my father's fury all the way to town. It was the first time I had ever felt sorry for a boy, and I began to sense that perhaps the war wasn't so much between male and female as it was between generations.

“Work, for the Night Is Coming”

WHENEVER I think of the word "work" I first think of my Aunt Clara. Next I think of the hymn we used to sing so often in our North Dakota village church:

Work, for the night is coming;
  Work through the morning hours;
Work while the dew is sparkling;
  Work 'mid springing flowers;
Work when the day grows brighter;
  Work in the glowing sun;
Work, for the night is coming,
  When man's work is done.

The logic of those verses has always eluded me, but their meaning has always been mysteriously clear, perhaps because I knew my Aunt Clara and so many others almost like her. Because I knew my Aunt Clara I am astounded at the number of people who seem to think of work as an abstraction – like truth or beauty. Sociologists, government experts, editors, commentators, union officials – even employers and employees – appear to be progressively more incapable of agreeing on a definition of the word "work."

I am not so rash as to rush in where sociologists fear to tread, and therefore I will not venture either into Webster's

Third New International or into a definition of my own. Instead I will invoke the example of my Aunt Clara, who was, beyond all doubts of committees and experts, a worker. Furthermore, she earned her fame as a worker within a milieu of competition that has never since been equaled: she was the wife of a North Dakota farmer when wheat was selling for thirty cents a bushel and no drought-stricken acre yielded more than eight bushels of smutty wheat.

Aunt Clara's only virtue, only vice, only reward, was work. Such dedication, of course, does not preclude a prodigious social life. I remember the nights when I was sent groggily late to bed, stumbling up the circling dark triangular stairs in a sorrowful departure from the light and gaiety of eight tables of whist going below. And I remember when those same card tables laden with feasts for the Ladies' Aid seemed to cover the whole vast bare yard between house and barn. Now that I have matured into a timorous hostess of three-couple dinners, I think I understand some of the sources of her widespread reputation as a worker.

She had her moments of levity. I will not forget the friendly birthday spankings she gave me (she was not a small woman), or the times she actually spat upon a new pair of shoes I was proudly exhibiting. (It was a Midwestern joke to spit on new shoes, but my Aunt Clara was the only person who ever made an honest aim. She had a most literal mind.)

Though we achieved a kind of understanding during the spanking and the spitting, I do not know exactly why I was sent every summer to spend two weeks on her farm, since I already lived on a farm myself — six miles away on the same dry, dusty North Dakota soil. My cousins and I were just the wrong ages for each other; the older one bullied me and the younger one provoked me. Thus I spent most of my visit following my Aunt Clara around the farm, and thus I observed Work in its pure form.

My own parents worked fourteen- and sixteen-hour days all summer, yet it always seemed that the household went to work at least an hour earlier at my aunt's. I remember a yawning and a shivering there that were not usually part of getting up at home on a summer morning. Certainly nobody stayed in bed once Aunt Clara was up. Everybody immediately set about doing something. Since it was far too early to set the table for breakfast (a hundred flies would have investigated every tine of every fork before we sat down to eat), there was only one thing for me to do besides swat flies, and that was to follow my aunt and uncle out to the morning's milking. At home I would have gone out to my swing in the grove, but there was no swing at my aunt's house.

They milked in the corral, because neither of them could be bothered to herd the cows into the barn unless the temperature had dropped below zero during the night. After nearly three decades have passed, I can still see my aunt — in apron, cotton stockings, Cuban heels, straw hat against the sun that would eventually emerge — striding into the corral, cornering a cow against a fencepost, balancing herself on a one-legged milking stool, butting her head into the cow's belly, and blasting streams of milk into a resounding pail — all within sixty seconds of entering the barnyard gate.

My parents used three-legged milking stools, and maybe that is why it seemed that my aunt and uncle worked so much harder. They couldn't take the time to sit while they milked eighteen or twenty cows. Work was much too serious to be sat down at.

Pail after pail came foaming to the cream shed, where it was hoisted high in Aunt Clara's dauntless arms and strained through cheesecloth into the separator bowl. But the pails were never heavy enough; the cows were not working hard enough.

It was the same with the dull red chickens scratching and dusting themselves in the fine black powder of their pen. When my cousins and I brought in the basket of brown eggs at night, there were never enough. What did those old hens *mean*, going into a lazy molt at this time of year? My aunt would go out there, come morning, and wring the neck of every molting chicken and can it up.

This was another small difference between my aunt and my parents. Neither my mother nor my father would wring the neck of a chicken. They used a sharp ax and the chopping block. But my Aunt Clara could not be bothered. She used simple muscle power. Work was work.

She finally met her equals in the garden. The weeds and the bugs worked as hard as she did, and she therefore hated them with the same stark emotion she gave to work. She rewarded their monstrous presumption with monstrous efforts against them; nevertheless, her acres of peas, string beans, navy beans, tomatoes, ground cherries, dill, eggplant, Swiss chard, spinach, beets, carrots, potatoes, sweet corn, radishes, onions, turnips, rutabagas, cucumbers, squash, pumpkins, lettuce, cabbage, gladioli, asters, and twenty other kinds of flowers were chewed up and choked out by what was, even in North Dakota, an appallingly outsized and colorful collection of inimical species. It was a juxtaposition of casualties in the garden war that revealed to me the compelling, awful, mysterious relationship between work and death that we sang about in church.

I was nearing the end of a long visit and trying to earn my keep as a seven-year-old by pulling the weeds around the plants while Aunt Clara hoed between the rows. Even for an endless North Dakota day, the afternoon was uncommonly hot. I wasn't paying much attention to the heat, though, because the day before I had found the biggest tomato worm in the world, and I was trying to hide him from my aunt till I could get him home. I kept him in a coffee can which I slid along under the tomato plants, ripping off a leaf now and then and dropping it down to him. I hadn't dared leave him at the house because my younger cousin would have stolen him to tease me.

He was at least five inches long and tautly fat, like an inner tube. His skin was a luminous green striped with white, and he had an obscene curving horn on his tail. He consumed enormous portions of tomato leaves and he deposited enormous turds on the shiny can bottom. I was leaning over him, protecting him from my aunt, when she cried out, "Oh, I can't see! Everything's black! I've got to sit down!"

She toppled backward, her legs sprawling, her flowered apron fluttering, her dress exposing gartered stretches of white thigh between stocking and corset. She lay gasping, her hand gesturing queerly till at last it found her eyes and covered them from the diligent sun. Her dislodged hat rustled nervously in the burning breeze, then sidled jerkily away down the row — as if escaping from a ghost.

My instincts were to follow the hat, but my brain failed to give the proper orders to my limbs. My head, like the sun, contained nothing except lucid flame, and the message came from the sun to me without words: Work is what you do till you die. When you can't see and everything goes black, then you have to sit down. Work, for the night is coming, when man works no more.

But it was obvious that the connection between work and death was much more subtle than a gross cause and effect, for presently my aunt sat up, pulled her dress over her knees, and sent me to fetch her hat and a dipper of water. She drank the water, pulled herself up with the hoe, reckoned the day was hotter than she had thought it was, and went on down the row.

I was afraid to stay with her and afraid to leave her to collapse again, all alone, and die out there of sunstroke. She would pause, lean on the hoe, breathe deeply, and rub the itching dark wet line her hat made on her forehead. "I can't understand it," she repeated. "Everything went black. I couldn't even see."

I crawled ahead of her up my row and rolled my worm out into hers. All the pairs of his blunt green feet scrabbled for cover, but he wasn't quick enough.

"Well, *I declare!*" exclaimed Aunt Clara, her merciless vigor restored. "I *never* saw a tomato worm the size of *this* one!"

She attacked, as she would have attacked a rattlesnake or a dragon. She raised her hoe, as I knew she would, and chopped my worm in halves.

As he squirmed out his preposterous green guts, I thought about how hard he had worked to digest all those leaves and now he would never be a butterfly. This was the last anybody would ever hear of him — unless my aunt should happen to tell my uncle about him that night at the supper table.

The work of one creature meant the death of another. The worm killed the tomato plant; my aunt killed the worm; the sun, in a manner of speaking, would finally kill my aunt. Work and death — two things equally ineluctable, equally significant, equally definite — so oddly connected in so many ways.

The Buggy on the Roof

IN 1934, the year of my memorable Halloween, nobody in Cleveland, North Dakota, had ever heard of trick-or-treating, that apologetic form of annoying neighbors, subsidizing candymakers, ruining teeth, upsetting stomachs, and cheating red-blooded human sprites. The contrast between what I did as a child and what my neighbors' children do now makes me embarrassed for them as they shuffle about in the brisk night under my porch light, dressed in the costumes of television cartoon characters, begging treats and also begging pennies for some admirable charity. (It would seem that every modern childish pleasure must have its "constructive aspects.") For my part, I would much rather participate in Halloween, now that age relegates me to the side of authority, by doing my best to scare the daylights out of somebody I can catch tricking me — the way I was scared by a drunken old man with the biggest shotgun in the world.

The children who come to my door will remember All Hallows' Eve as the night when they sold their right to rebellion for some sugar in expensive wrappings. I think they ought to remember it instead as a night when they worked off a good deal of normal anarchy before it could do them or the rest of the world too much damage — the way I did as a third-grade anarchist.

That year, perhaps because I felt I was outgrowing the

talk of my classmates in our three-grade primary room, I had taken to eavesdropping on the conversations of my elders. For at least three weeks before Halloween, I would hear the big boys in the eighth grade talking at recess about how they were going to "fix old Englehart and old Merry." Mr. Englehart was the strong-armed principal of our twelve-grade school, and Mr. Merry, as dour a Scotsman as ever bore the name, was the vice principal and teacher of the seventh and eighth grades. Gloria Merry, his daughter, was my best friend in the third grade, and nobody could have been more impatient to see what was going to happen to her father than she was. Since I lived on a farm some distance from town, she invited me to spend the night with her, and my mother innocently consented to my celebrating Halloween with my "little friends."

Gloria's brother Walter was two years older than we, and he formed a tenuous link between us and the big boys. He knew, for instance, that a group of them planned to meet down at the abandoned livery stable around seven o'clock, and thither we went as soon as we could escape the supper table. The sun had set more than two hours before, and it was very dark and very cold. It was too early for the great harvest moon, which rose conveniently late that night. We startled the plotters when they discovered us skulking at the heavy, splintered doors, but they allowed us to come into the stable. One of them advanced upon us ferociously, his face eerie in the glow of the flashlight he held, and said, "You know what'll happen to you little kids if you get caught? They'll put you in jail. And if they put you in jail and *torture* you till you tattle on us — well, you just better stay there, that's all. Because if they let you out after you tattle on us, we'll just kill you, see? So just don't get caught, that's all."

I am a little nostalgic now, in this big world, for his conviction that in a town of less than three hundred souls there would be no ideas about the identities of the persons who had rigged buckets of water to fall at the touch of a hidden trigger, who had rocked privies off their foundations or switched the signs from the pool hall and the Community Methodist Church.

The boys had spread out around them the homely tools of mischief – the long wires, nails, hammers, pliers, string, flashlights, paraffin saved from the tops of their mothers' jelly jars, knives for cutting a clothesline or carving out insults to the grownup world, and tin cans filled with rocks for making a farewell noise after the damage was done.

Opportunities sat waiting and vulnerable in the night. Even the two or three families who had indoor toilets had privies too, in deference to self-conscious guests. There were the town pumps, which would wear their handles high in the air the next morning – creatures built literally in the manner of Joyce Kilmer's trees, each with a disjointed arm languishing above a dried-out, rasping leather throat, pressed against the earth's nonflowing breast. The buckets of priming water would be overturned, and the parents who first came to use the pumps, having forgotten what morning it was, would have to trek back home to get the last quart of water from the pail by the sink. And there were the windows, some of which would still show wax the next spring. For we *did* use wax, not soap, and I would rather look back on the two or three good wax jobs I have done than on any number of store windows painted innocuously with tempera under the patronizing eye of a "cooperating merchant."

We stowed away the equipment and flitted off into the blackness. There were no street lights, and the only sounds we heard were those of our careful feet on the wooden sidewalks. Except for the pool hall and the service station out on the highway, all commerce ceased at six o'clock, and the boys knew that all the downtown businessmen would be at home finishing their suppers. By the time we had fixed up the restaurant, the dry-goods store, the blacksmith's shop, my greatuncle's hardware store, the post office, and the old car in front of it, the night was far enough advanced so that we could undertake more ambitious projects with minimum risk. We headed across the tracks to the Merrys' house.

The boys made Gloria and me stay at the barn door when they went inside. We could hear the sounds of creaking floorboards and of iron-rimmed wheels rolling over straw. Out they came with the Merrys' tattered buggy. They pulled a few fistfuls of wiry stuffing from the leather seats and tossed it at us. They had already propped a couple of stolen planks from the ground to the roof of a lean-to shed adjoining the barn, and now they boosted the buggy up the planks, ran it up the long steep barn roof, and set it astride the high ridgepole. In silent hysterics they clambered backward down the roof, slid off the planks, and shouldered them for use on old Mr. Englehart's barn.

But Englehart, being better paid than Merry, had a sturdy lock between us and the buggy in his barn. And his privy had, of all things, a new cement foundation. We had to content ourselves with waxing his basement windows and stretching a wire at shin height between his kitchen door and his prudently reinforced toilet.

As we headed for the scattering of houses along U.S. Route 10, we saw the dim yellow bulb still burning above the two rusty pumps of Gerry Schlosser's Super Service Station. Reasoning that where there was light there might be action, two of the boys slithered into the ditches on either side of the highway, telling the rest of us to stay back and keep quiet. We did not have long to wait. Old Gus Koch came weaving down the pavement, seeking more beer and fresh company now that the pool hall had closed. He shambled into the wire they were holding, staggered, recovered himself with the lucky oscillations of the drunk, and began screaming oaths into the empty night.

Schlosser ran out of his station, and Gus fastened on his arm. "Carnsarn it, Gerry! Can't nobody do nothing about them kids!"

"I'll shoot the carnsarned brisshes off their carnsarned buttsh!" cried Schlosser. He ducked into his two-by-four office and came out with a shotgun. He waved it around in the light of his little yellow bulb, but he did not leave the station. He had no idea of where we might be, in all that great blackness of prairie, nor of how many more wires might be stretched out in the darkness.

We were safe, but the boys could not let the challenge pass. We waited until the two old men had squeezed themselves back into the tiny office, and then we headed for the privy fifty feet behind the station. Every year it was a little shakier. This year it offered scant resistance. It whined and groaned as the boys rocked it back and forth, and suddenly its one vital prop fractured with a terrible noise.

Schlosser rushed out with his shotgun just as the privy slumped down across its own ditch.

The boys vanished, Gloria's brother along with them, and we were left running so far behind them that we had the nightmare feeling of not moving at all. The gun exploded in our direction — once, twice. Then again, when we thought surely we were safe — crash, *crash!*

Those shots were the loudest sounds I have ever heard in my life, and they seem to have driven from my memory any recollection of how we got together again with Gloria's brother, or what we told her angry parents we had been doing.

I do, however, remember perfectly the wonderful satisfaction I felt when I saw pompous Mr. Merry's shabby buggy silhouetted on top of his barn in the cold morning light of All Saints' Day.

The buggy stayed there for at least a week, till Mr. Merry could round up enough friends to help him get it down again, and for all those days the force of Mr. Merry's personality was quite neutralized by the craven attitude of his buggy, tensely clamping the ridgepole of his barn between its thin-spoked wheels, shuddering with acrophobia in the November gales.

The King's Birthday

ALL THE Christmases of my childhood were deeply involved with the doings of the Eldredge Community Methodist Church in Eldredge, North Dakota, and all but one of them now, two decades later, are blended together in my memory. I cannot recall which year it was that I sang "Away in a Manger" all by myself, wringing the skirt of my new made-over dress in both hands so that I had it up around my thighs by the time my solo was over, or which year I was an angel and dripped hot wax from my candle on the wrist of a shepherd kneeling before me, or which year I was the Virgin Mary and had to have Wilbur Becker for a husband. But I remember the year I was the Christmas Elf because we did things so differently that time, under the direction of Miss Ellen Kretchmer of New York City. I haven't really thought about her in years, and I wonder if she, wherever she is, thinks about Eldredge as Christmas comes around.

She was the new primary school teacher in 1934, the year that I was in the second grade, and on the first day of school, when we were telling each other about ourselves, she explained that she had left her father and mother far away in a place called Queens because all the little children in Queens had more teachers than they needed, but the little children in Eldredge would not have had any teacher at all if she had not come out to us.

I suppose Miss Kretchmer arrived in Eldredge the way any other stranger did – aboard the Northern Pacific passenger train, which hissed to a resentful pause once a month or so, discharged a passenger or two, and rushed off again into the hypnotic distance. There was little of Eldredge that she could not see from the depot platform. The most impressive part of the skyline, for those whose skylines must go up and down to be impressive, was Rex Beahr's grain elevator, which rose a hundred feet above the thousands of acres that fed it and looked out hungrily upon them like a god waiting for the autumn sacrifice.

The only building of consequence not visible from the depot was the Eldredge Community Methodist Church – the hub of Eldredge. But that deficiency was more than compensated for, since Miss Kretchmer went to live at my great-aunt's house, which was just across the road from the church. Every day Miss Kretchmer could look out of her bedroom window at the splintered wooden sidewalk in front of the church, the dying tree in the parched yard, the pointed yellow windows and scaling clapboards of the façade, and the squat steeple with its ragged shingles wilting in the sun.

Even after I had fallen in love with Miss Kretchmer, as we all did, it took me a while not to be nervous around somebody who smiled so much. The other grownups I knew didn't seem to have much reason to smile. She was very young, but I didn't know that then. I knew only that she was as splendid as one would expect a person from a place called Queens to be. Her shoes were shiny and high-heeled, her skirts were many-tiered, and her coat had fur on the collar, but her most remarkable raiment was her own vitality. Her mouth and cheeks were red and her hair was thick and black. Compared to her, every other grownup I knew seemed all the same color, like a wheatfield.

The remarks I overheard about her scarcely registered in my mind; I had already accepted the fact that adults were almost certain to be disgruntled about anything that was important to children. There were people who said she ought to be got rid of right away for telling us stories about other parts of the world, mostly New York. But the major complaint was that she never went to church. That was especially galling to my greataunt, who was proud of her strategic location and had never boarded a teacher before who had failed to take advantage of it. "She doesn't have an excuse in the world," my greataunt would say. "Here she is, right across the street from it." Miss Kretchmer was definitely breaking a precedent by neglecting to put in at least a token attendance. The minister, being the best-educated man in town, was traditionally elected to be head of the school board, and the separation of church and state did not exist in Eldredge. Thus it was that Reverend Adams's wife came plowing across the street through a late October snowstorm to have coffee with my greataunt one afternoon, and between them they decided that the best way to draw Miss Kretchmer into the church was to give her some responsibility so she would feel that she belonged.

The most natural thing to do was to put her in charge of the Primary Department's annual Christmas program, and by the time she got home from school the two ladies were so excited about it that they went out to greet her as she stood on the back porch brushing the snow from her overshoes. She had hardly finished setting the overshoes on a newspaper near the stove to dry, drawn off her leather mittens, and shaken the snowflakes from her coat before she was committed to the church. It was settled that she would practice with us in the basement of the church on Sunday mornings while the service went on upstairs. That way Miss Kretchmer would be seen at church and no child whose parents were *not* in church would get a chance to be in the Christmas program.

Miss Kretchmer sent off to New York for a Christmas play. As soon as it arrived we began learning the songs from it, sitting in the narrow circle of heat around the coal furnace and straining to hear her above the noise of the fire and the minister upstairs. She often had a cold and she would hit a hoarse note, clear her throat, find the note on a pitch pipe, and start over again. For any other Christmas program we had ever given we had just brushed up on songs we'd known all our lives, like "Silent Night," and then learned parts that were pretty much the same from year to year. But the songs in the play from New York were quite different, and they were so hard I used to practice all the way home from church. I would sing something like:

North or South, Black or Yellow—
We all love the jolly fellow
Who sets all our hahts to sinGing
With the pretty gifts he's brinGing.

Then one of my grandmothers in the front seat of the car with my mother would stop talking and turn to me and say, "You're not saying your words right." "I'm saying them just like Miss Kretchmer told us," I would answer. "She says to be very careful to all sing it just the same way." But why were we singing about North and South and Black and Yellow anyway? Because, I explained, the name of the play was *Christmas Over All the Earth.*

"Well, I swan," said my mother's mother. "Does that sound like a church program to you, Ida?"

"No, it don't," said my father's mother. "Somebody ought to just look in at what that girl's doing down there in that basement."

But nobody did look in on what was going on in the basement, because anybody who would have had any authority did not want to get involved with helping to put on the Christmas program.

Everybody realized too late that there was to be no second-grade Madonna cradling a heavily swaddled doll, no third-grade Joseph pleading with an innkeeper, no nursery chorus of angels entangling themselves in each other's tinsel-edged wings, no shepherds wearing their older brothers' bathrobes and mumbling a poem in unison while a teacher in the front pew hissed at them to look at the star. We had learned all the songs, we had taken home patterns for costumes, and our mothers had already begun struggling with grass skirts and white bonnets like the one on the Old Dutch Cleanser can.

One could not fully appreciate the magnitude of Miss Kretchmer's error without knowing that only three important things happened in Eldredge every year and that they always happened a certain way. There were May Day, the Fourth of July, and Christmas Eve at the church. Important as the first two were, they were mightily overshadowed by the third. Everybody in town and all of the farmers for a considerable distance around came to this Christmas Eve service. There were even quite a few Russian Seventh-Day Adventists whose garlicky presence in our church and clamorous grabbing after the gifts were annoying proofs of their lack of pride. The Christmas program had been the same as far back as anyone could remember: the minister read the first seventeen verses of the second chapter of the Gospel according to Saint Luke, the congregation sang carols and watched the Sunday school pupils perform a version of the Nativity, and then the minister appeared in a Santa Claus suit and passed out popcorn balls and red net stockings filled with peanuts and hard candy and an orange at the toe that was the only orange a number of us would see during the year.

Then Miss Kretchmer committed an additional sacrilege by importing Neva and Ivan Koslov — Russian and Seventh-Day Adventists — to be the little Spanish children. Miss Kretchmer explained to the members of the cast that we were short-handed, and besides, the Koslovs looked more Spanish than any of us. A stunned incredulity was the only thing that prevented some kind of explosion.

Two days before Christmas my mother left me in my greataunt's kitchen while she bought groceries and (I tried not to hope too much) perhaps some other things I had brought to her attention. I thought that kitchen was about the most wonderful place on earth. It was almost as big as our whole house, with its many windows and its high ceilings and cupboards all the way up the walls.

Now all the rooms in the tall house were filled with the Christmas perfumes of fruit, candy, greens from Minnesota, and pink gummy syrup boiling in the kitchen. As the Ladies' Aid members arrived they were put to work making popcorn balls and wrapping them in waxed paper or scooping peanuts out of a rustling gunny sack and dropping them into the mesh stockings with the oranges in the toes. I was so bemused by the rare gaiety in the room that I kept forgetting it was my job to answer the door.

Mrs. Jennings was irked at having to knock three times, and she swept past me in massive impatience. She glared up the stairs and called over her shoulder into the kitchen, "Is that girl here now?"

"No," my aunt shouted back over the din. "She's over practicing all her *dancers* today, with the piano."

"Well," said Mrs. Jennings, stamping into the kitchen and fixing my greataunt with a furious eye, "did I ever tell you, Elsie, that Mae ain't even going to have *a word* to speak this year? Not one word! Last year she said a four-line pome and she was only five. This year that teacher told her she thought Mae would make a good Dutch girl for a pantomime, and all Mae is going to do is clump around the stage in some wooden shoes this girl dug up somewhere and 'set them out for Saint Nick.' And so I'm supposed to learn her to look shy and hopeful instead of learning her a pome. What kind of a program is this when half the kids don't say a piece by themselves? Last year *all* the kids five and over said *something!*"

Before anybody could act sympathetically indignant, Mrs. Halstad burst out: "Well, you know what *I* have to do—*I* have to paint Carl's face yellow with some stuff that girl give me so he'll look like a Chinaman. What do you think of *that?* Painting a boy's face all up on Christmas Eve. I thought it was going to be Carl's turn to be Joseph this year. I tell you, I'm just so mad about it I just don't care whether he's in the program or not." She jerked back to the stove and yanked the long spoon through the bubbling syrup while the steam collected in big drops on the bristles above her lip.

On Christmas Eve I held the box with my costume in it on my knees as we drove into town, so I could bend down and listen to the bells jingling through the green and red folds. I sneaked into the Sunday school side of the church, which was reserved for the participants. The girls were changing their clothes behind one of the screens we used for separating the Sunday school classes, and the boys were behind the other. The boys kept running past the girls' screen and snatching off the dresses and petticoats draped over the top of it. The girls kept screaming and Miss Kretchmer kept shouting, "Boys! Boys!" She was perspiring so much that some pimples showed through the red of her cheeks. None of the grownups had come to help, and Miss Kretchmer was trying to do all the dressing and the lining up by herself.

An overflow crowd was jamming the vestibule and Reverend Adams stalked through the chaos, sweating in his dour black suit and hauling his watch out of his vest pocket every two minutes. Miss Kretchmer looked up frantically from a rip she was pinning in Neva Koslov's skirt and motioned me to go on. I ran out to the rail of the chancel, stopped and saluted the audience with my cap the way Miss Kretchmer had shown me, and launched the evening with a brisk monotone recitative that went something like this:

I'm the jolly Christmas Elf,
I'll bring to you much mirth.
When I wave my wand you'll see
Christmas over all the earth.

Then I pulled the curtain — three sheets basted together and hung from a pole supported at either side of the chancel by a hatrack — so the audience could see Christmas in Norway. Back and forth I went with the curtain and my frenetic verses, while Christmas lumbered over the earth.

As nervous and young as I was, though, I could not escape the awful knowledge that would have been apprehended by any performer of any status and any age — the audience was lost and had been lost since the performance began. For this one night the folk of Eldredge wished to live in that unbounded empire of belief where everybody understood the same miracles and nobody concerned himself with the idiosyncrasies of countries and colors, but only with the Birthday of the King. They wanted to see again the same gentle mystery, peopled by the same shepherds and angels and kings, accoutered with the same settings of mangers and tinfoil stars, and animated by their own thin little imperfect children, sober-faced over their great responsibilities. And because we were not communicating to them anything they were prepared to receive, they had nothing to share with each other, so they sat crowded against one another in the same sad isolation that ruled the rest of their scattered lives.

They sat that way, that is, until the entrance of Neva and Ivan Koslov caused them to stiffen together in unanimous disapproval. The Spanish dance scarcely got under way before it became obvious that Miss Kretchmer's rushed repair job had not remedied whatever it was that ailed Neva's skirt; it circled painfully lower and lower on her hips and then swirled down to a gaily colored rumple around her ankles. Ivan looked at his sister standing in a woeful petticoat in front of a churchful of people and vanished from the stage. Neva was too disorganized to do anything at all. For a very long time there was no sound in the church.

Then suddenly laughter blew into the hall like a fresh wind, tentative at first, and then abandoned and compulsive. This was the first credible thing that had happened all evening. There stood a "Roosian" kid in dirty underwear, just like the other little Russians they saw running about half clothed in dusty farmyards milling with squawking chickens and starving dogs. They laughed in vast relief from the strain of trying to believe in anything so far removed as the wet lushness of an African jungle or the yodeling ebullience of an Alpine village, and even though Miss Kretchmer sent in Mae Jennings and I heard her wooden shoes thundering behind me, they kept right on laughing, and after I saw that it was all right I laughed as hard as anybody else. Only when all of us had laughed away all of our disappointment did the sound release us to gasp sheepishly and wipe our eyes.

The laughter had united us all in righteous camaraderie. We even forgot our grudge against the Seventh-Day Adventists for coming to our church and getting in on the Christmas treats that had been made two days before in my greataunt's kitchen.

Miss Kretchmer must have left shortly after Reverend Adams came out in his Santa Claus suit shaking some sleigh bells and yelling, "Ha, ha, ha" as he handed out the presents. At any rate, I didn't notice her in the vestibule as we passed into the bitter night, where we paused, shivering, to point out to each other the Star of the King of Love – hanging over Eldredge just the way it had once hung over that other little town in Israel.

❦❦❦❦ The Cold Wave

MY FATHER and grandfather would often speak of the earlier days in North Dakota—of the strong man who could swing a hundred-pound sack of wheat to his back by flinging it over his shoulder with his teeth, of tornadoes that switched the roofs of barns and houses, and of hailstorms that rained sheep-killing stones, heaping July wheatfields with desolations of ice.

Even more fascinating to me were their stories of the early winters. I would never see any winters like these, they said, for a new and milder weather cycle now prevailed. I would never know the bitter years that built the grim legends of our northern land.

My mother used to tell me how once a prairie wolf had stalked her as she walked home alone from school, over miles of abandoned stubble. I always felt cheated when I looked at the faded photograph of my father sitting on a horse, his hat higher than some telephone wires. He had ridden that horse right to the top of a gigantic snowbank, packed so hard that the horse's hoofs hardly dented its crust. It was true that there was usually a bank in our yard that reached to the top of the clothesline pole, but this was hardly satisfying when I knew what grander things had been. Why couldn't something happen after I was born, I wondered.

Yet when the sort of thing I was waiting for finally came,

its coming was so natural and casual, so unlike a legend, that I mistook it for a part of the routine of my existence. It was part of my routine, for instance, to run over behind the depot with some of the town kids and slide on the ice by the tracks before I went over to Schlagel's Store to get a ride home with my father. I was almost always the only girl to go sliding, and it was also part of my routine to try to beat the boys to the smoothest patch of ice. On the day I am talking about, the only departure from routine was that there were no contenders for any of the ice.

I didn't slide very long myself, because I began to feel some undefined discomfort that an adult would have easily identified as a deeply pervasive chill. But when an eight-year-old is too cold, he will first feel oddly tired and lonely and deserted, so that he will go to find people. Thus it was that although I began to have the feeling that I had played too long and that surely my father would be waiting for me angrily, when I opened the door to Schlagel's Store I saw by the big Sessions clock that it was still only a quarter of four and that I would have to wait for him.

Several amorphous large men were warming their hands at the stove in the center of the room and speaking to each other in Russian. Their faces were always very red, and Mr. Buskowski's purplish, large-pored cheeks frightened me a good deal, as did his heavy teasing in a broken English I would make terrified and ineffectual efforts to understand. I managed to sneak past them all to the rear of the store where the harness and great quilted collar pads hung from brass pegs screwed into rough boards. Julius Schlagel's clerk, Irma, was back there shoveling some shingle nails into a brown paper bag. She straightened up the nail bin, stared at me, and stepped nearer to see my face under the hiss of the gas lamp. "You want to know something? You froze your face, kid."

"How could I? I just came straight over here from school," I lied.

She gave a skeptical glance at the clock and said, "Go get some snow and fetch it in here."

I brought a mittenful of snow and submitted to her harsh massage. The snow felt hot on my cheeks, so I knew I'd frozen them all right.

"Now don't go out again, hear?"

Except for the candy counter, the store was a dark monotonous jumble of bags and boxes and barrels. I was hungry, so I diverted myself by studying the penny candy and deciding how I would spend a penny if I had one. Since I rarely had the penny, no one paid any attention to me. When I did have one, I would tap it nonchalantly on the grimy glass case — not as though I was impatient to be waited on, for indeed I was not, but just to let Irma and Julius know that I was a potential customer, an individual to be treated with respectful attentiveness when I had finally made up my mind.

Since I had no penny, I was glad to see my father come through the door. He saw that Julius was listening to the radio and he strode brusquely past me to ask him about the weather reports. Julius dispensed about as many weather reports as he did bags of flour and corn meal; in 1935 in drought-ruined North Dakota, radios were a luxury, like candy.

Without speaking, Julius turned up the volume so my father could hear the announcer. ". . . the Canadian cold wave is pressing southward from central Manitoba and is expected to hit northern North Dakota tonight, causing substantial drops in the temperature within the next twenty-four hours. This is KFYR in Bismarck . . ."

"Forty below in Winnipeg last night," Julius said to my father.

"You been out in the last hour? I bet it's thirty below here right now. The pump's froze solid. We gotta go thaw it out." Directing his last sentence to me, he turned and made his way past the Russians, nodding uncordially.

The sun had set while I was waiting in the store, and a vast gloom in the sky sagged low over the town weighting the rigid streets with cold. The heat absorbed by my snowsuit was gone instantly, and my thawed-out cheeks stung badly. My father scuffed me up over the brittle heaps of snow at the curb of the wooden sidewalk and hoisted me into the sleigh. The sleigh was a wagon box transferred to runners for the winter. I wanted to stand up, but he made me sit on the old Indian blanket spread on straw. There were hot stones under the straw. Then he draped a cowhide from the high side of the wagon box down over my head.

Though I could see nothing, I could hear my father talking to the horses and I knew he was wiping the frost of their own breathing from their nostrils. Beneath me was the thin scrape of the runners, then the rattle over the railroad tracks and smoothness of fields of snow. The cow hairs made my nose itch and the straw poked at my legs. It was very dark.

Finally my father stopped the sleigh by our house and lifted me out. "Tell Mother I'll be in directly, soon as I unhitch," he said.

Despite the hot stones, my ankles were numb, and I tripped and fell as I ran to the house. My lip struck the gallon lard pail I used for a lunch bucket and stuck there. I lay tense and still in the snow waiting for it to stop sticking. Once my little sister caught her tongue on the pump handle because she wouldn't believe me when I told her it would stick. She jerked away in fear and tore bleeding skin from the tip of it. So I waited until I could feel the warmth of my breath free my lip before I moved.

The porch timbers creaked with cold, like thin ice. I could hear my mother yelling to me to get the snow off my clothes and to shut the door tight even before I opened it.

The top of the kitchen stove glowed gray-red through its iron lids, and the belly of the big round stove in the living room seemed stretched dangerously thin, as though it would surely melt soon and spill out flaming coal on the floor. My mother had set the kerosene lamp on the warming-oven doors above the stove so she could see how much salt to put in the potatoes. I could smell the rabbit she was roasting in the oven for the dog.

My father came in the door, stomping snow clear across the kitchen, and demanded a teakettle of boiling water. Seeing that I still didn't have my snowsuit off, he told me to come with him to work the pump handle.

While he poured the boiling water down the pump, the steam rushing up into darkness, I struggled to free the handle, but I couldn't budge it. Even when he grasped it in his large thick leather mitten it didn't move. "Well, it looks like we'll have to melt water for the stock. Take this back to the house." He handed me the teakettle.

I was glad we had to melt snow for water, because then my little sister and I could play a game called Eskimo. We stood on chairs, balancing ourselves imprudently near the searing surface of the stove to lean over the tub. As soon as the dry snow had melted a little, we began to mold the figures for an Eskimo village – Huskies, people, babies, igloos, polar bears, and walruses, just like the ones in *The Book of North American Mammals* that my mother had got once in a set of books from the National Geographic Society. We conducted hunts and dogsled treks and sent the Eskimos into the water to harpoon the seals that were languidly floating there. But as the water warmed, the seals disappeared, and it was death for the harpooners to go into the sea. While the shores of their iceland slipped away into the ocean, the frantic people moved higher and higher on the iceberg mountain. Perched on its slushy sides, they would see a small hole appear in their snow island. Then the sea would gush up through the hole, the island would break in pieces, and the ice people would fall into the fatal warmth. Just as the warm wave washed over my people, the game would become hideously real to me, and I would often have nightmares in which I was climbing, climbing, on an ever-collapsing mountain to escape a hot tide.

After supper my father set out for the barn with two pails of the snow water. I had to spend about a half hour, it seemed, getting my outside clothes on again so I could carry the lantern and open the barn door.

I was well acquainted with the shock of stepping from the warm kitchen into a winter night. But none of the freezing memories of the past could prepare me for the burning air that night. It was like strong hot smoke in my nostrils, so that for one confused instant I thought I was going to suffocate with the cold that was so cold it was hot. I gasped for breathable air, and my father said, "Don't do that! Breathe through your nose — your breath is warmer that way when it gets to your lungs."

We walked carefully down the hill to the barn; then I slithered down the steps chopped in a snowdrift in front of the door and slid it open. The barn was very old, but always before it had been warm with the heat of the animals kept in it all day long. But that night, being inside didn't seem to make any difference. I still had the kind of ache in my temples and cheekbones that I always got when I took too big a mouthful of ice cream. The cows shifted and swung their tails and wouldn't stand still to be milked. My father poured some milk into a pail and told me to feed it to the little new calf in a pen at the rear of the barn.

He had arrived out of season and was not yet two weeks old. Usually by the time the calves came, the mothers were outside all day, and both mothers and calves quickly got used to the idea of being separated. But we had been keeping all the stock inside for nearly a week, and neither cow nor calf was properly weaned. She lowed to him and he cried back to her; he was still determined to nurse. He was still stubbornly bucking and shoving his nose all the way to the bottom of the bucket, and desperately bunting the side of it when he got a noseful of milk. I liked him, though. His hair was almost as fine and soft as a human baby's, and he had a white star on his gleaming black forehead.

Although I had never seen cattle shiver, the little calf looked as though he was shivering as he advanced stiff-legged to our evening battle with the pail. I braced it against my shins and waited for him to begin bunting. At least a winter calf didn't damage you as much as a spring calf did; at the moment I was well padded with long underwear, two pairs of long stockings, and thick pants. I patted him between the ears and he sucked my fingers with his rough, strong tongue.

After the milking was done, we lugged the pails and lantern up the hill and started back for the barn with more water. In two more trips our toes felt numb and thickened, and we both had frostbitten faces. I had the two white spots on my cheeks again and my father's high thin nose stood out bloodless against the chapped red of his face. We took a last look at the stock; there was nothing more we could do. There was no way to heat the barn and the cows were already half covered with straw when they lay down. We rolled the door shut.

In the house we planned for the night ahead. My little sister and I would sleep in one bed, with all the blankets and quilts in the house over us, and my mother and father would use the feather tick we had rolled up in a little storeroom we called the cubbyhole. When we opened the door of that little vault to get the tick, the frigid air pushed out across the living room like a low dark flood against our legs.

It took a long time to warm the tick and blankets from the unheated bedroom at the stove. We would hold them as close as we could to its hot belly, but as soon as the warmed section was moved away it grew cold again. We left the bedroom door open, but though the living room grew instantly colder, the bedroom grew no warmer. While we were making the beds we puffed white clouds at each other across the mattresses. We heated our two sadirons and wrapped them in towels, one for each bed. Then my father stoked both stoves full of coal and we got under the piles of bedding.

My sister and I lay close together, our legs bent and our toes touching the wrapped-up iron. Partly because I couldn't get warm and partly because I was worried about some things, I couldn't go to sleep. I wanted to know what a cold wave was. In the long solitude of prairie childhood I had memorized two sets of books — the set from the National Geographic, and a set called *A Childhood Treasury* that contained legends of many lands, my favorites being those from Scandinavia. How could it possibly be that so many things had happened before I was born? For instance, *The Book of North American Mammals* told of a time when the plains of Russia and of North America had borne glaciers a mile deep. And before the glaciers there had been vast herds of mammoths. There was a drawing of them lifting their shieldlike foreheads against a gray horizon, marching on tall shaggy legs over the frozen tundra — tundra that had once covered our wheatfields. The book told about how before the glacier finally came, the weather had gotten colder and colder, so that the mammoths had to grow longer and longer hair.

But even with their long hair and clever trunks and sixteen-foot tusks curved in unlikely tangles of bone, they had been unable to defend themselves. Why? Under the picture it said that a herd of these mammoths evidently had been preserved intact for centuries, and that one of the discoverers had even tried eating the meat of a carcass thousands of years old. Why couldn't the huge and powerful creatures have run away? It must have been some kind of flood, I thought, like the flood we had in our garden after a cloudburst, only different and much bigger — a flood that could race with the speed of liquid one moment and turn completely solid the next, locking forever the great knees bending for another battling step, then the tusks fending off masses of debris, and finally the long trunks flailing above the tide in search of air. A cold wave freezing so fast that the bubbles of their last breathing would be fixed like beads in the ice.

What if some polar impulse was now sending a flood to rise up out of the north, to flow swiftly over our house, becoming ice as the wind touched it, shutting us off from that strangling but precious air above us? I had heard of digging out of a house completely covered with snow — that used to happen in the days before I was born — but did anybody ever dig out of a glacier? I wanted to go and climb in bed with my mother and father and have them tell me that it wouldn't get to us, that it would stop at least as far away as Leeds, twenty miles to the north. But the last time I had tried to climb in with them they had told me not to be such a big baby, that I was a worse baby than my little sister. So I lay there wondering how far the cold had gotten.

Finally the morning came. I could look from my bed across the living room and into the kitchen where my father, in his sheepskin coat, was heating some water saved from the melted snow. The tub, refilled after we had emptied it for the stock, was standing in the corner of the kitchen next to the door. The snow in it was still heaped in a neat cone. It was odd to think of a tub of snow standing inside our house, where we had slept the night, and never feeling the warmth of the stove a few feet away — to think of how the tiny flow of air around the storm-lined door was more powerful than the stove filled with coal.

I felt the excitement of sharing in heroic deeds as I pulled on the second pair of long wool stockings over my underwear and fastened them with the knobs and hooks on my garter belt. I was not going to school because it was too cold to take the horses out, so I was to help with the barn chores again.

The cattle were still huddled together in their one big stall. My father set down the pails and walked swiftly to the rear of the barn. The little calf was curled quietly against the corner of his pen. The black-and-white hairs over his small ribs did not move. My father climbed into the pen and brushed the straw away from the sleeping eyes, just to make sure.

I stood looking at the soft fine hair that was too fine and the big-kneed legs that were too thin, and it seemed to me that I now understood how it was with the mammoths in the Ice Age. One night they had lain down to sleep, leaning ponderously back to back, legs bent beneath warm bellies, tusks pointing up from the dying tundra. The blood under their incredible hides slowed a little, and the warmth of their bodies ascended in ghostly clouds toward the indifferent moon. There was no rushing, congealing wave; there was only the unalarmed cold sleep of betrayed creatures.

A couple of nights later, over at the store, the men talked of the figures Julius had gotten over the radio. There had been a dozen readings around fifty degrees below zero. Fifty-two at Bismarck, fifty-eight at Leeds, and sixty-one at Portal on the Canadian border.

"My termometer is bust before I see him in the morning!" shouted Mr. Buskowski. "I do not even from Russia remember such a night."

Hopelessly studying the candy counter, I realized that even my father had forgotten the stiff little black-and-white calf in the contemplation of that remarkable number. "Sixty-one below!" they said over and over again. "Sixty-one below!" The men didn't need to make legends any more to comprehend the incomprehensible. They had the miraculous evidence of their thermometers. But for me that little death told what there was to know about the simple workings of immense catastrophe.

❦❦❦❦ The Water Witch

BENJAMIN the water witch lived in a dark little shed attached to the rear wall of his grandnephew's blacksmith shop, with a layer of clotted sawdust for a rug between him and the boards that served as a floor. For his purposes the sawdust was better than a rug, because he shook too much to be very accurate with his coffee-can spittoons.

Besides the day-long din that would have maddened almost anybody but the person making it, Benjamin had to bear the bitter cold of the shed in winter and a heat like that of Leroy's forge in the summer. But if he hadn't been Leroy's greatuncle he might not have had any place at all to live, and anyway the temperature of the air around him obtruded only vaguely on the world he lived in. All year round, the cuffs of his one union suit flapped about his wrists and flared over the tops of his ankle-high shoes. Sometimes, during those drought years in our little North Dakota town, when the thermometer under the awning of the barbershop was hovering around a hundred degrees, old Benjamin would take off his blue work shirt and reveal the scalloped lines of sweat creeping like a lava flow down the chest of his underwear.

In a time of general affliction, a creature who is even more afflicted than the rest is either shunned and feared as the most disfavored subject of the gods, or else esteemed as the possessor, through his unimaginable misfortune, of a special purpose in life. When that creature is a water witch in the midst of an unprecedented drought, it is not hard to see why he should be sought after, if not accepted or understood. Thus it was that after a lifetime of being supported by the parched but unpatronizing charity of the community, the old man was elevated, in his last years, to a status of full self-support.

Even the Russian immigrants who scarcely spoke English knew that staring, palsied Benjamin was their last hope. In a universe so populated with inimical forces, it seemed reasonable that a few creatures of malign aspect were in fact good spirits in disguise, waiting only for a demonstration of belief in the goodness under their bestial exteriors to unleash that beneficence upon the believers. Mythology is full of tales of such creatures. Hardship and ignorance made the myths, and they are still revived and leaned upon whenever people cannot get along without them.

Like most other people, I have gotten my water out of a faucet for a long time now — a faucet that presumably is connected to a limitless supply of water — but I still experience a vestigial terror of being waterless if for some peculiar reason no water comes out of the faucet. It is like a racial memory of desperate hunts for water. Such desperate hunts went on over millions of square miles of the breadbasket that was becoming the Dust Bowl in the fourteen summers of desolation.

There are poems, sometimes written by people riding a train from one ocean to the other across that stricken expanse of the continent, which celebrate the pathos of a house abandoned in the blowing fields, but I have never seen a poem which deals with the day on which a child of that house is sent out for a half a bucket of water and comes running back through the dust to report that the well is dry.

The hunt for wells was so intense that in 1931, when the drought was only seven years old, the government of British

Columbia employed a Cornishwoman named Evelyn Penrose as its official Government Water-Diviner, and sent her into the homesteads in the Okanagan Valley, where she often found herself as far as ninety miles from a place where there was enough water for a bath. There were many other instances, in those days, of the hiring of dowsers by official agencies. It is not surprising that Benjamin, who offered the added persuasion of an affliction, should have been catapulted to eminence in our little dying town.

Even so, I don't think my father believed in water-witching, and I don't think he asked old Benjamin to come out to our half-section. I was six years old then, three years younger than the drought, which had dominated my life like a cruel unnatural stepsister out of a fairy tale. We had been living with my grandparents after a depression business failure, and were continuing to live with them until we got the new place in shape and found water. However, my father and I happened to be on the farm for a special reason the day Benjamin came shambling down the rutted lane that connected our farm to the county road. He must have heard at the blacksmith shop that we were planning to dig a well, and simply assumed that we would be waiting for him. A passing neighbor had given him a ride from town, but, in an inarticulate graciousness, did not offer to go out of his way for him, pretending that a quarter-mile walk for a spastic was no more than for anyone else. Benjamin came just as we were slamming the door of our new home against the raging fumes of the sulphur we had set in cans on a stoked-up stove – the way we fumigated for vermin in those pre-DDT days. We planned to stay the day to make sure the house didn't catch fire, so my father had a little spare time in which to indulge the water witch (if that was indeed the way he looked at it). I tagged after them all morning, partly because I was afraid of the deadly house with the awful gases swirling around its insides, and partly because I did not want to lose sight of my father while a creature like Benjamin was around. His twitching lips drooled tobacco juice, his lower eyelids sagged away from the red-lined globes of his eyeballs, and his hands fluttered from his buttonless shirt sleeves in a terrible anarchy. A high, stumbling voice came out of his massive chest, and his clothes and shoes were heavy with the deep fine dust of the land in which he proposed to find water.

He mumbled repetitiously about veins and depths, which his missing teeth rendered into "depfs," shuffling over the fields, with us at a patient pace behind him. He held his Y-shaped branch high, straight out from his chest like the drummer in the American Legion band. Suddenly the branch in his hand flipped over and the tail of the Y pointed rigidly at his feet. He had had such an odd grip on the branch that when it flipped over it appeared to have thrown both his wrists out of joint. He began to shake much more violently.

"It's right below me here!" he cried. "There's a lot of it — a whole lot — I can tell by the way it's pullin' at me — it's just like it was taking the stomach right out of me. It's close or it couldn't do like that — depf of eighteen feet, not more. Set a stake here quick, I tell ye — it's rilin' my stomach to stand here."

My father obediently drove a stake down through the billowing dust into the hard earth beneath the palsied branch. Then he said coaxingly to the old man, "Do you feel up to following this vein along for a ways, Ben?"

"Well, I dunno what you want that fer," he said in pleased complaint, "but if you think I can find something even better than what we've got right here I reckon I can try — but I tell ye this is hard on a man. It's mighty hard on a man."

The old man "followed the vein" down the hill to a spot under a huge elm tree where his dowsing rod, green as it was, cracked loudly in its wrenching somersault. He stood there transfixed, while the leaves of the great tree above him quivered in the wind and flickered darts of light over the wavering lines of his body.

Crowded as my world was with invisible beings and magical forces, I had never expected to be an actual witness of supernatural energies at work.

Even my father jumped a little, but he recovered himself quickly enough to say a little too loudly and nonchalantly, "Well, now, Ben, I think you did it! I reckon I ought to dig right here, don't you?"

I thought that was about as superfluous a question as he could have asked. The kind of power that had just been demonstrated to us could have called all the water in the world to that spot under our elm.

My father did dig there. He found no water until he had gone three times as deep as old Benjamin's rod had said, but finally the sand began to whisper and slide in around him as he spaded it into the bucket my grandfather cranked up and dumped aside, and then the water began to seep up around his legs and to fill faster than he could bail and dig. After we got the pump installed and the water had a chance to clear, we realized that we had a well bordering on the miraculous. The water was wonderful. Most wells in that area yielded water so strong with minerals that it was often almost as unpotable as it was good for the teeth. When old Benjamin tasted the water from our well he trembled in pride, and my father gave him five dollars out of gratitude to the earth.

As the drought became worse that summer, we came to see what a remarkable well we had. I, of course, accepted both the unusual taste and abundance of the water as the natural result of Benjamin's water-witching. I was sure that he had not just found that water, but had an absolute control over keeping it there. As soon as we had transplanted the vegetables that we had started indoors while we were staying with my grandparents, we began hauling water from the well up the long hill to the garden. My father would hitch the team to the stoneboat, load an oil drum on it, empty a dozen buckets into the drum, then flick the reins with a specious optimism at the sweating horses. Their mosquito-covered thighs vibrated with effort as they yanked and dug for footing to move the first inch that would jolt the loaded sledge out of its inertia. When they had finally dragged and scraped it to the top of the miserable incline, my father would pour the water, bucket by bucket, into the trenches along the garden rows, and then drive the weary animals back down the hill to get another load.

For weeks the well supplied us and our stock and our flourishing garden, while all around us the wells of neighbors began to go dry. The water table receded from one sputtering pump shaft after another, and men went shamefaced and frantic to their friends, who became suddenly aloof and cautious. There was, after all, nothing anybody could barter for water – not seed wheat or labor or even money. People who had lived for three generations under the homesteaders' law of unconditional hospitality to those in need now began to live under another law – the law of the desert – the law that had caused the wells of Isaac to be called such names as "Hatred" and "Contention." None dared to ask for more than enough to water their animals and themselves. Their winter's vegetables, begun in the hopeful boxes of earth propped against kitchen windows looking out on March snow, faded into dead yellow strings lying in the dust of their gardens. If Benjamin could not find new wells for them, there was nothing left for them to do but slaughter their bony milch cows, take the proceeds from their lugubrious auctions, and go West.

The heat wilted even the wind, and the normally restless windmills stood mute against the silent sky, while the water in the great tanks below them evaporated through a covering of green scum. I was so hungry for water that I could bring myself to play in one of those round wooden tanks, and I still remember climbing into it and scraping my heels and calves down against the hairy growths on its sides. The tank was in our neighbor's horse pasture, and my mother would take us there in our old Ford, driving across the hard useless fields, and would then sit in the shade of the car reading the Jamestown *Sun* while my three-year-old sister and I jumped and paddled about in the lukewarm mixture for a hour or so. Then we would come home and sponge off the green that coated our bodies and matted our hair.

At night, ten minutes in bed was a long time — long enough for a person no bigger than I to have searched out every unslept-on cooler piece of sheet, and to have made the whole bed as hot as I with my searching. Every night was like the worst two days of the measles.

But despite my miserable nights I had no way of knowing that things were worse than usual. I was making a bird-nest collection and I spent my days visiting various bird homes, admiring the eggs, then the baby birds, and finally taking the nests for my own when the birds were done with them. My favorites were the twin doves who hatched in a nest built every year in the same place — on top of a low stump in the center of a mound so charmingly furnished with hundreds of tiny toadstools that there was no doubt it was the dancing ring for the fairies who belonged on our farm. Since my sister was too little to be of any real interest, the birds and the shy beings that only the birds ever saw were the sole companions of my long summer days and the only recipients of my wistful affections. They absorbed me utterly, and they could make me forget the worrisome conversations between my mother and father that I could hear every night after I had been put to bed.

But then came the three days of heat. The thermometer in the shade of our porch registered one hundred and twelve degrees at one o'clock in the afternoon of the first day. So unobtrusively that we never knew exactly when it happened, eleven of our fattest hens drew their last breaths through beaks straining away from their hard dry tongues and slumped into the hollows they had made while dusting themselves, as though they had dug their own graves.

That was also the day that our well finally betrayed us. We used up all the priming water in the can by the watering trough and then we brought down the last of the water we had in the house, but all we heard was the rasp of sand in the shaft. My father put four barrels on the wagon and drove the team to town, three miles away. There they would allow him only three barrels at a time, afraid the supply would not hold out. The stock required all the water he could get, and the garden, after only one day of such punishment, contracted a mortal thirst.

The next morning there was still no water, but I visited the first nest on my route as usual. I could barely see the three-day-old babies under their undulating blanket of gluttonous red ants, their frail necks drooped comfortingly across each other's backs and their little heads swollen with the blue bruises of their eyes under the lids that would never open. During those first two days the whole generation of nestlings in our north and south windbreaks perished and their parents disappeared. Only the twin doves on the enchanted stump survived, for their mother's throat made milk as well as lullabies, and they drank and were spared the crawling red feast.

There was still one more day of heat and then we had the

cloudburst. The irony was clumsy, but the meteorological principles behind it were perfectly sound. We crouched in the earth-floored cellar while the wind tore at the splintered wooden door over us and the tornado ripped apart a barn and a house a few miles to the south of us. Then the sky that had been so hot and dry and far away lowered itself to our roof and spilled out the flood that removed the last skeletal traces of our garden. It seemed to me that all the water in the world, after disobeying the water witch for three days, had come back to us through the sky. There was more water than anybody could have imagined without believing in magic.

Still, the damage was local enough not to be mentioned in the newspapers of places any farther away than Fargo. It just happened that nine years of drought, three years of depression wheat prices, and the treason of a well had exhausted our capacity to exist any longer in an environment which offered no semblance of cosmic hospitality. Even our meek-hearted doves decided to leave.

Thus it was that we joined the caravan of destitute nomads who sought the western ocean, where the people had no experience of the perfidy of wells and therefore concluded that our difficulties must be the result of a lazy shiftlessness. They called us Okies if we had come from north of Texas, and Arkies otherwise, and generally treated us the way people with such names would expect to be treated.

Perhaps it was only the depression that made so much depend on so little. I know I was not clear, at the time, as to whether the drought made the depression or the depression made the drought. Even now I don't know whether it is nomads who make the desert or the desert that makes nomads. I do know that a lone man trying to wrest consistency out of the prairies can be tragically out of scale. Only nomads can live in the wastelands of sea, sand, ice, or dust, where the figures of men are forever out of scale.

If we had all been birds, we could simply have forgotten

a lost generation and migrated to the next nesting site. If we had been Indians, we would be there still, having followed the buffalo, which would have followed the grass that was sure to be green enough somewhere, for there is usually a greener valley for people to find, if only they are not encumbered by the idea of human permanence.

Since we were not nomads by nature, we were obliged to shrink on the outskirts of the small group of farmers at our auction, who made humiliating bids on the sad trappings of our permanence and bought them at sums that made my mother's eyes seek my father's in frightened dismay. We had counted on getting much more to help us move to another place where there would not be so many enemies of roots.

Inexplicably the veins of several wells old Benjamin had dowsed were renewed after the cloudburst, and the desperate people, renewed in their faith, came ever more frequently to the blacksmith shop. They would bring in a singletree that was about ready to be welded or a horse that was about to lose a nail, and then they would drift back to the corner where Benjamin sat propped against the wall on a cracked anvil draped with gunny sacks. The drought had promoted him from his shed into the shop. A man would start to speak of how the east forty was a little dry, and he was thinking of spying out a vein to open there. Softly and casually they spoke, as people will to a being who might be easily offended because of his terrible affliction and the pride it takes to bear it. They spoke as people do to a being who may be cajoled into bestowing on suppliants who hit upon the proper ritual a stay of execution, a drink of real water out of a mirage.

My father and I saw Benjamin the water witch for the last time — sitting on his anvil, trembling and rolling his eyes, whittling aimlessly on the tail of a dowsing rod — on the day we went down to Leroy's shop to get a little welding job done on the wagon box we were converting into a trailer. We didn't mention anything to him about the well, or even tell him why we were there in Leroy's shop, because we too bore our affliction with pride.

When the Fields Are Fresh and Green

The boy moves through his life, keeping a shy
Watch on the man who now assumes his face.

— Douglas Nichols
Johnny Appleseed

WHILE WE ARE growing up, we become more surprised every year that we seem to other people to be changing, because to ourselves we seem always to be the same. And even while we exult in the higher mark on the closet door where we are measured every year, we feel an increasing apprehensiveness that a day will come when we will seem to have changed so much that nobody will remember who we are.

Thus, when we are still very young, we sense that our first memories of ourselves constitute the only reality by which we will always understand our existence. The problem is that nobody ever seems to see anything the same way we see it, and therefore the memories by which we place ourselves in time and space can never be verified by anybody else. This is the loneliness and the terror of childhood — not to see things the way anybody else sees them, not to understand why some things are "real" and some things are not.

My first hazy memories of myself were set nearly two thousand miles from the place where my second, verifiable memories of myself began. My father's business failed in 1931, and my family moved from Seattle back to a desolate half-section in North Dakota just before I was four years old. At that age, I would, in any case, have begun slipping from my first dreamy existence into my second "real" existence, but it was the drastic change of place that seemed to me, over the next few years, to have been the cause of all the changes in my existence. I had one possession that unequivocally connected me with all the parts of that first existence — all the parts I couldn't remember, all the parts everybody agreed that I remembered, and all the parts I alone was sure I remembered. That possession was a doll with opening and closing eyes that I got for Christmas in Seattle the year before we moved. I took her with me wherever I went, and frequently she got left at the weather end of a long prairie trek when I had gone looking for something — gone out to watch in the haunted cloudless morning and found only beautiful emptiness. After a few years the poor doll's face grew pale under the prairie sun, and lined with the fine cracks of excellent crockery. But still she had the same delicate brows, the same private smile of a baby who knows she will never have to grow up.

I made a special point of taking her whenever my mother and I went to see Edith Bagley and Edith Bagley's mother, because when we went there I really needed company. Edith and her mother had a dark high parlor filled with dark high furniture that I had to climb up into but that I must never touch with my feet. After Edith and her mother and my mother had all watched me and my doll get settled without doing any damage, they left us to ourselves. Edith and my mother had gone all through school together and then through college together in Jamestown. Then they had come back home together and my mother had married my father and Edith had not married anybody. But Edith was talented in a number of ways. My mother always played the piano for her when she sang a solo, and usually when we went there it was so they could practice something.

In one corner of the parlor was a table that was covered, when Edith was not using it for her work, with an ecru lace tablecloth that hung down so that all you could see of the table was its four massive clawed feet flexing themselves over the roses on the carpet. The chair next to the table had lions' heads at the ends of its arms, and the lions were roaring without making any noise. It was clear to me that furniture like that could come alive at night when people were asleep, and I always tried to act wide awake when I was in a roomful of it. I wiggled and cleared my throat and did as many things as I could without having somebody tell me to sit still.

In another corner of the parlor sat old Mrs. Bagley, who did not, like the furniture, look as though she might be alive. The top part of her was gray and white with sweater and hair and skin and cloudy spectacles. The bottom part of her was gay in the way a new grave is gay — all covered with spots of color woven from wilted flowers over a shockingly high mound. The mound of her under the festive mosaic of her afghan was appalling because you couldn't imagine a regular body under there, with a stomach and hips and legs. What *could* have been under that afghan? Only once did I see any part of a body. Hanging below the multicolored yarn fringe was a brown cotton stocking that bulged far out over the top of a black, high-heeled shoe tied with tasseled laces.

The parlor smelled of a half-century of dust and cooking and of about twenty years of Edith's painting. I would sit in one of the great chairs, watching every minute to see that I didn't touch any part of any wooden animals, and try to think of something to say in case I was called upon to admire Edith's painting. It seemed to me unclean to paint flowers and thistles and twisting vines all over plates and cups that people were supposed to eat from and drink out of. I always felt a little sick when Edith answered the door in her smock, because I knew the smock meant she was painting dishes, and if she was painting dishes, I would have to say something.

Edith weighed almost three hundred pounds. That was what gave her wonderful volume when she sang. Her face was round like a plate, and it had a finger wave for a frame — just like the tendriled edgings on her plates. She had soft boneless hands, but they were facile and clever, as weak hands often are.

One day I watched them work for a long time. They were making artificial lilies for Easter Sunday in our church. The claw-footed table was heaped with piles of wire, stiff threads with yellow nodules at one end, fuzzy orange things shaped like tiny cattails, squares of green and white paper of the consistency of snakeskin, needles, thread, pliers, and instructions. Edith picked up one of the long wires in one of her limp hands. She twirled a strip of stretchy green paper around the wire. "See!" she said. "Now we have a stem!"

After hard study of her diagrams, Edith produced an Easter lily. It had long pointed petals of snaky white paper and enormous reproductive organs made of the threads with the yellow nodules at their ends. All the thread ends and all the petal ends were wired together at the center of the lily, and all the wires were neatly hidden in a calyx made from a little green wax cup. Then she made a calla lily, so she could try out the fuzzy orange pieces that looked like cattails. I don't know how many lilies she made before my mother came back from grocery shopping. All I know is that a sentence started repeating itself in my head. It was a simple imperative sentence, and one I had made a point of memorizing after reading the story it was in. "Stop, Little Pot, stop!" That was the magic command that nobody could remember for days and days after the obliging Little Pot got set off by some idiot who knew only the starting words and not the stopping words. The picture with the story showed the town's whole population eating pathways with teaspoons through the streets of waist-high mush.

Like the porridge nobody knew how to turn off, Edith's lilies inundated the little Community Methodist Church on Easter Sunday. Lilies jammed the vestibule, the aisles, the altar, the pulpit, the windowsills, the hymnal racks. Guarded by my mother on one side and my grandmother on the other, sitting in a safe church pew, I sank into that familiar lonely terror: everybody else's eyes were seeing something that mine could not see. To everybody else those things of wire and resinous snakeskin paper were flowers.

The year of that Easter was the hardest my grandmother and grandfather and all the other people on the prairie could remember. It was colder and windier and drier and hotter and dustier. When the meager harvest was in, Number 1 wheat sold for twenty-six cents a bushel. Finally a bleak frigid December brought the long year to an end. My mother told me not to expect much from Santa Claus. I'd given up believing in Santa Claus long before, and I know she must have known that. But it was less painful for both of us to pretend that it was Santa Claus who was poor.

That was the first time I had ever done any pretending of the kind that grownups did, and it gave me, oddly enough, that same feeling of lonely terror I had when I realized that I must be seeing something that nobody else saw — or that everybody else must be seeing something I couldn't see. I began to understand that most people simply decided on what they wanted to see and then saw it. They decided on what they wanted to believe and then believed it. And everybody pretended to believe what everybody else pretended to believe so that they could talk to each other. Santa Clauses ringing bells on the street in Jamestown did not believe in Santa Claus. Edith Bagley did not believe in her snakeskin lilies. They were all trying to make reality better for everybody else. And they were all trying to explain themselves to each other in order to try to make themselves more real to each other, in order not to lose each other. But the harder they tried to make the world real for each other, the more hopelessly they separated themselves from each other. It was even more lonely to be *deciding* what was real than it was not to have any idea of what might be real and what might not.

It made me feel very old — to believe in Santa Claus because I decided to believe. From then on, I would be responsible for what I saw and what I believed. I would make the decisions that created my existence and the decisions that created the world. The more I succeeded in believing what everybody else believed, the less real anything would be, because the things that are the most real are the ones that surprise us the most, and when everything must be decided upon and agreed upon, nothing can surprise us any more. We can never be surprised by the color of the grass or the color of the sky, and so they can never be quite so bright as they were in that first existence, when we were always being surprised.

And just at that time when I needed her the most, my dearest proof of that other existence, my faded cracked Baby Dimples, disappeared. I looked everywhere for her, but I did not admit to my mother that she was missing. I was afraid I had left her outside on the wrong afternoon and she had been buried under a five-foot snowdrift. If I asked about her, my mother might exclaim, "Oh, *dear!* You *didn't* leave her out on the day we got that awful blizzard, did you?"

There was also the possibility that my mother had allowed her to fall into the grubby eye-poking fingers of my little sister while I was away at school learning about reality. Then my doll would be like most of the other dolls I knew. At best she would have one eye stuck open and the other stuck shut. At worst, the whole mechanism would be turned over in her head and the only thing that would show through the eyeholes with their painted lashes would be a steel bar with rubber bands attached to two dull metal balls (the backs of the glass eyes) suspended in an empty china skull, rolling up and down, opening and shutting in hollow darkness. If she had suffered such an attack, and was now on some closet shelf until my father could find time to try to fix her, I didn't want to know about it.

I was pretty sure, though, that I must have left her outside. I spent a few dusky afternoons digging deep into the most likely snowbanks. I knew I wouldn't find her; I just wanted to show her or somebody that I felt as bad as she did about her being down there under the suffocating whiteness.

I still hadn't found her when Christmas came. That Christmas morning was the bleakest in my memory. There was no towering pungent tree like the ones from that other existence where Christmas trees grew on all the mountains, in all the parks, and beside all the houses. There was instead a tiny tree that had lost all its perfume while coming hundreds of miles from Wisconsin or Michigan. And under the tree, as gaily wrapped as if our decisions and our agreements and our responsibilities could always be made as beautiful as surprises, were sleepers and mittens and stockings and underwear – things I had been doing without during the first part of that bitter winter so that I could get them for Christmas. And, of course, because I needed them and because I was grown up now, I pretended that they mattered.

It seemed to me that our little family would suffocate from pretending in our little house that was so crowded by our little tree – like my doll under the snowbank. But my mother gave me a portentous look, as if to say that she knew you couldn't have Christmas without surprises and that nobody expected you to. She slipped out of the house and came back with a bundle in her arms – a bundle just the size of a new baby, swaddled in a precious furry pink blanket. The Christmas surprise! The Surprise that creates a universe of surprises every time it is born. She lifted a corner of the blanket so I could see the baby's face.

It was dead. It must have died while she left it out in the car, waiting to surprise us. Its cheeks were purple, like the cheeks of people found under snowbanks after blizzard snows have melted. Even its closed eyelids were purple.

"It's Baby Dimples!" my mother cried happily. "Santa Claus took her away and made her all new for you!"

I looked at the dead face again and saw around it the pen-like scrolls of Edith Bagley's plates. On the delicate brow and cheeks I recognized the dusty purple paste that Edith Bagley managed to use, in one spot or another, on all the dishes and cups she painted.

"Isn't she pretty now?" my mother pleaded. "You left her outside and she got all cracked and faded. Now look at her pretty red hair! Look at her healthy cheeks!"

I couldn't have said it to myself then, but I understand that even the master artificer which, in my little world, Edith Bagley was, could never bring surprise from one existence to another. Shock (a word I didn't know then, though I knew the feeling) no doubt was transferable; surprise was not. The glad surprise of a very young child that morning has come, that the grass is green and the sky is blue — and all without any decisions made by the child — that glad surprise, I have now come to understand, is what we beg our artificers for, pay them enormously for, especially at Christmastime. But they, being part of the grown-up conspiracy to decide what is real, being, like the rest of us, helpless members of the second existence, no longer know, any more than the rest of us, what is real — what is surprising.

I say that I understood this, and the way I know I understood it is that I knew I was making a statement about my existence when I said to my waiting, heartbroken mother, "Yes, my baby is much prettier now."

I was careful, after that, to tuck my doll into her crib every night, and to do it when my mother was sure to see. Since I never took her out of the house with me again, it wasn't hard to find her to do the tucking in. There had been nights when even the long summer prairie evenings had caught me in the dark, with the panicked sounds of hard-pressed fecundity all about me and the weight of the heavy-leaved black boughs over me — there had been nights when I risked my life to search for her in the grove, so I could bring her safely home and put her to bed, grieving and promising never to forget her again. But in our second existence we don't grieve and promise with the same unqualified passion with which we grieve and promise in our first existence. We remember, in our second existence, how forgetful we are.

And so, now that my last proof of my first existence had been transformed into the first proof of my second existence, I no longer had to seek her or grieve for her or make promises to her. She was always there in her crib, with her purple cheeks.

Something important happened in the town that winter, not long after Christmas. Somebody got married or, more likely, somebody left for the West Coast and had a party in the town hall before they went. If a family was going to sell out, it was that time of year that would make them decide. Christmas and New Year's over. Nothing to look forward to but snow till April. No commitment to a crop planted. Winter feed for the stock about gone, because of the last summer's drought. Not much cream to sell and not much of a price for what cream there was. A time of year when the Pacific Coast temperatures, printed in the Jamestown *Sun,* seemed unbelievable. It didn't seem to matter where you were during these depression years. After you'd been in one spot for a while, you decided things couldn't be quite so bad anywhere else, and so you moved. My own family had gone from North Dakota to Seattle and back, and we were destined to go again to Seattle in another couple of years.

At any rate, something important happened in the town and Edith sang for it. I still hated her so much that I could barely speak to her when we went to her upstairs house so she and my mother could practice the songs she sang. I sat in the chair with the lions carved on its arms and listened while they went over and over the songs, but only one of the songs said anything I could understand, and that's why I still haven't forgotten it.

Edith stood by the piano, her smock trembling over the vast regions where her emotions echoed and re-echoed themselves, until she herself must have lost track of them and could believe only what everybody believed — that she had, as compensation for her appalling obesity, for her appalling mother, for her appalling loneliness, a great voice.

Another thing I cannot forget (and this is one way you can distinguish your first existence from your second: never in your first existence do you wish you could forget anything) is the painful difference between herself and the girl she sang about, as she stood, wide as the piano, at the high-note end of the keyboard upon which my little mother played. The song she sang, the one I can't forget, had these words:

The roses all have left your cheek —
I've watched them fade away and die . . .

Oh! I will take you back, Kathleen,
To where your heart will feel no pain,
And when the fields are fresh and green,
I'll take you to your home again.

I know I understood that Kathleen was not ever going to see the fields again, because the song made me cry. It was the first time any song had affected me that way. I sat in the lion-headed chair where I had once watched Edith make the lilies with no perfume, holding my fists against my eyes, horrified at crying over something as silly as a song — especially the kind of song that Edith Bagley would sing — and even more horrified that somebody might catch me.

If anybody could go back, if Kathleen could have gone back, then nobody would cry over the song, but almost everybody does. We cherish our griefs over those green fields because our griefs seem to prove that what we grieve over must once have existed. It is good that all of us have these griefs. They do not separate us as do our beliefs.

Now that I am grown, I have discovered that our second existence does bring us one surprise — love. Now that I have children of my own, I try, as my mother did, to save their first existences for them, even though I know it is impossible. All the generations of us will go on forever trying to save the green fields for each other and we will always fail, but because it is for love that we try to do what is impossible, we redeem our second existence.

And in a way none of us ever really leaves those fields that made us. It is from those lost fields that we go on shyly, silently calling to each other. It is from those fields, forever sealed against the trespasses of our grownup selves, forever splendid with light falling like trumpet salutes through the old heavy boughs of the world, that each of us keeps his long watch on the people who come to assume his face.

Children of the Harvest

ON A SUFFOCATING summer day in 1937, the thirteenth year of drought and the seventh year of depression, with our mouths, nostrils, and eyes full of the dust blowing from our bare fields, my family sold to our neighbors at auction most of the accouterments of our existence. Then we loaded what was left into a trailer my father had made and drove West to find water and survival on the Washington coast.

During the auction the two classmates with whom I had just finished the fourth grade hung about the desultory bidders giving me looks of respect and undisguised envy. They envied me not so much for the things they could imagine as for the things they couldn't — the unimaginable distance I was going and the unimaginable things along it and at the end of it.

And though we all could have imagined most of Montana well enough, how could any of us have imagined an end to the prairie's limitless sky and the giddy encroachments rising higher and higher against that sky that were the Rocky Mountains? How could we have imagined how in burning summer the forested profiles of the Cascades could echo everywhere the shouts of white falls above us and green rivers below? Who could have imagined, once confronted with their gray expanse, that the waters of Puget Sound were not actually the Pacific, but only a minute stray squiggle of it? Who, finally, could have imagined that there were so many people in the world or that the world could offer them so hospitable a habitation?

There were so many things I could scarcely believe even when I was doing them or looking at them or eating them. We lived in a cabin on an island for a few weeks after we arrived, and it always seemed impossible to me that we could be surrounded by so much water. I spent every moment of the hour-long ferry trip from the mainland hanging over the rail gazing down at the exhilarating wake of my first boat ride. The island was exactly what any island should be — lavish green acres covered with woods and orchards and fields of berries, ringed by glistening sandy beaches richly stocked with driftwood. Once in North Dakota my aunt had brought a very small basket of black cherries to my grandfather's house, and I had made the four or five that were my share last all afternoon. I would take tiny bites of each cherry, then suck the pit and roll it around with my tongue to get the faint remaining taste, till it came out as clean and smooth as a brook-bottom pebble. But on the island I would climb into the trees with my five-year-old sister and have contests with her, seeing which of us could get the most cherries in our mouths at once. Then we would shoot the wet pits, no longer hungrily scoured of their slipperiness, at each other and at the robins who perched above us. Sometimes I would go into the fields with my mother and father and spend an hour helping pick raspberries or blackberries or loganberries or any of the other things they worked in, but there were really only two important things to do — play on the beaches and eat fruit.

It didn't occur to me that things would ever be different again, but one day early in August the last berry was picked and we took the ferry into Seattle, where we bought a big brown tent and a camp stove. We added them to our trailer load and drove back over the green-and-white Cascades, beneath the glacial sunrise face of Mount Rainer, and down into the sweaty outdoor factory that is the Yakima Valley. There the Yakima River is bled for transfusions to the millions of rows of roots, its depleted currents finally dragging themselves muddily to their relieved merger with the undiminishable Columbia. One can follow the Yakima for miles and miles and see nothing but irrigated fields and orchards — and the gaunt camps of transient laborers.

The workers come like a horde of salvaging locusts, stripping a field, moving to the next, filling their boxes or crates or sacks, weighing in, collecting the bonuses offered to entice them to stay till the end of the season, and disappearing again. They spend their repetitive days in rows of things to be picked and their sweltering nights in rows of tents and trailers. We pitched our tent beside the others, far from our pleasant island where the owners of the fields were neighbors who invited my sister and me among their cherry trees. Here the sauntering owners and their bristling foreman never smiled at those children who ran through the fields playing games, and only occasionally at those who worked beside their parents.

In North Dakota I had worked on our farm — tramping hay, driving a team of horses, fetching cows, feeding calves and chickens — but of course that had all been only my duty as a member of the family, not a way to earn money. Now I was surrounded by grownups who wanted to pay me for working, and by children my own age who were stepping up to the pay window every night with weighing tags in their hands and collecting money. I saw that the time had come for me to assume a place of adult independence in the world.

I made up my mind I was going to earn a dollar all in one day. We were picking hops then, and of all the rows I have toiled my way up and down, I remember hop rows the most vividly. Trained up on their wires fifteen feet overhead, the giant vines resemble monster grape arbors hung with bunches of weird unripe fruit. A man who does not pick things for a living comes and cuts them down with a knife tied to a ten-foot pole so the people below can strip them off into sacks. Hops don't really look like any other growing thing but instead like something artificially constructed—pine cones, perhaps, with segments cleverly cut from the soft, limp, clinging leaves that lie next to the kernels of an ear of corn. A hop in your hand is like a feather, and it will almost float on a puff of air. Hops are good only for making beer, so you can't even get healthily sick of them by eating them all day long, the way you can berries or peas.

Pickers are paid by the pound, and picking is a messy business. Sometimes you run into a whole cluster that is gummy with the honeydew of hop aphids, and gray and musty with the mildew growing on the sticky stuff. Tiny red spiders rush from the green petals and flow up your arms, like more of the spots the heat makes you see.

The professionals could earn up to six dollars a day. One toothless grandmother discouraged us all by making as much as anybody in the row and at the same time never getting out of her rocking chair except to drag it behind her from vine to vine. My father and mother each made over three dollars a day, but though I tried to work almost as long hours as they did, my pay at the end of the day would usually be somewhere between eighty and ninety cents.

Then one day in the second week of picking, when the hops were good and I stayed grimly sweating over my long gray sack hung on a child-sized frame, I knew that this was going to be the day. As the afternoon waned and I added the figures on my weight tags over and over again in my head, I could feel the excitement begin to make spasms in my stomach. That night the man at the pay window handed me a silver dollar and three pennies. He must have seen that this was a day not for paper, but for silver. The big coin, so neatly and brightly stamped, was coolly distant from the blurred mélange of piled vines and melting heat that had put it into my hand. Only its solid heaviness connected it in a businesslike way with the work it represented. For the first time in my life I truly comprehended the relationship between toil and media of exchange, and I saw how exacting and yet how satisfying were the terms of the world. Perhaps because of this insight, I did not want the significance of my dollar dimmed by the common touch of copper pettiness. I gave the vulgar pennies to my little sister, who was amazed but grateful. Then I felt even more grownup than before, because not everybody my age was in a position to give pennies to kids.

That night I hardly slept, lying uncovered beside my sister on our mattress on the ground, sticking my hand out under the bottom of the tent to lay it on the cooling earth between the clumps of dry grass. Tired as I was, I had written post cards to three people in North Dakota before going to bed. I had told my grandmother, my aunt, and my friend Doris that I had earned a dollar in one day. Then, because I did not want to sound impolitely proud of myself, and to fill up the card, I added on each one, "I'm fine and I plan to pick again tomorrow. How are you?"

I couldn't wait to get to the field the next day and earn another dollar. Back home none of my friends would have dreamed of being able to earn so much in one day. The only thing to do back there for money was to trap gophers for the bounty; and even the big kids, who ran a fairly long trap line and had the nerve to cut the longest tails in half, couldn't make more than twenty cents on a good day, with tails at two cents apiece. I earned a dollar and forty cents the next day and the day after that, and at least a dollar every day for another week, until we moved to another place of picking — a pear orchard.

By that time it was September, and most of us children from the rows of tents stood out at the gateway of the camp and waited each day for the long yellow school bus. I had never seen a school bus before, and my sister and I were shy about how to act in such a grand vehicle. We sat together, holding our lunch buckets on our knees, looking out at the trees beside the roads, trying to catch a glimpse of our mother and father on the ladders.

The school had about three times as many pupils in it as there were people in the town back in North Dakota where we used to go to buy coal and groceries. The pupils who were planning to attend this school all year were separated from those who, like me, did not know how many days or weeks we would be in that one spot. In our special classes we did a great deal of drawing and saw a number of movies. School was so luxurious in comparison with the hard work I had done in North Dakota the previous year that I wrote another post card to Doris, telling her that we never had to do fractions and that we got colored construction paper to play with almost every day. I copied a picture of a donkey with such accuracy that my teacher thought I had traced it until she held the two to the window and saw that the lines were indisputably my own. After that I got extra drawing periods and became very good at copying, which always elicited more praise than my few original compositions.

I was understandably sad when we left that school after two weeks and went to Wenatchee. For the first time, we were not in a regular camp. The previous year my father, recognizing that the crops had not brought in enough to get us through the winter, had taken the train to Wenatchee after the sparse harvest was in and picked apples for a man named Jim Baumann. Baumann wanted him back, so he let us pitch our tent on his land not far from his house. We made camp, and after supper Baumann came down to talk about the next day's arrangements. The school was not so large as the other one, and there was no school bus for us because we were only a half mile away from it. Baumann was shorthanded in the packing shed and needed my mother early in the morning. Besides, there was no reason why she should have to take us to school, because he had a daughter in my grade who could walk with us and take us to our respective rooms.

"Why, isn't that lovely!" my mother exclaimed with unwonted enthusiasm. "Now you'll have a nice little girl to play with right here and to be your friend at school."

Her excitement was rather remarkable, considering the dubious reaction she had had to everybody else I had played with since we started camping. It hadn't seemed to me that she had liked even the boy who made me a pair of stilts and taught me to walk them. Now here she was favorably predisposed toward somebody I didn't even know. I agreed that it would be nice to have a nice little girl to play with.

The next morning my sister and I sat on the steps of the Baumanns' front porch, where Barbara's mother had told us to make ourselves at home, waiting for her to finish her breakfast. We had already been up so long that it seemed to me we must surely be late for school; I began picturing the humiliating tardy entrance into a roomful of strange faces.

Two of Barbara's friends came down the driveway to wait for her. They both wore the kind of plaid skirts I had been wondering if I could ask my mother about buying — after all, she *had* said all my dresses were too short this fall because of all the inches I'd grown in the summer. The two girls looked at us for a moment, then uncoiled shiny-handled jump ropes and commenced loudly shouting two different rhymes to accompany their jumping.

Barbara came out on the porch, greeted her friends with a disconcerting assurance, jumped down the steps past us, insinuated herself between them and clasped their hands. "I have to show these kids where the school is," she told them. Turning her head slightly she called, "Well, come if you're coming. We're going to be late." Swinging their arms together, they began to skip down the driveway.

A couple of times on the way to school they stopped and waited until we got near them; I yanked irritably on my little sister's arm and thought about how her shorter legs had been holding me back ever since she was born. I always seemed to be the one who had to drag a little kid along.

The teacher kept me standing at her desk while she called the roll and started the class on a reading assignment. When she looked up at me, I got the irrational impression that I had already managed to do something wrong. She asked where I had come from and I said "North Dakota," thinking it would be simpler than trying to tell all the places I had been in the last three months. She gave me the last seat in a row behind a boy in dirty clothes. As she passed by him she made the faintest sound of exhalation, as though she was ridding her nostrils of a disagreeable smell.

At recess a boy in a bright shirt and new cream-colored corduroy pants yelled "North Dakota, North Dakota" in a funny way as he ran past me to the ball field. The boy who sat ahead of me came up and said confidentially, "We been out all around here for two years. We come from Oklahoma. We're Okies. That's what you are too, even if you didn't come from Oklahoma." I knew I could never be anything that sounded so crummy as "Okie," and I said so. "Oh, yeah!" he rejoined stiffly. I walked away before he could argue any more and went to find my sister, but the primary grades had recess at a different time, so I went and stood by the door until the period was over. That afternoon I stayed in my seat reading a history book, but the teacher, who seemed to want to go outdoors herself, said, "It's better for the room if everybody goes outside for recess." So I went out and stood around the fringes of two or three games and wondered what was funny about North Dakota. Somehow I had the feeling that it would hurt my mother if I asked her.

The last part of the day was given to a discussion period, when each of us who wanted to was given a chance to tell about an important day in his life. The important days of my classmates, all about having a part in a play or learning to ride a bike, seemed so pathetically juvenile that I was impelled to speak. I stood at my seat and told about how before we had gone to the pear orchard, which was before we had come here, I had earned a dollar all in one day in the hopfields.

From two sides of the room Barbara's friends turned to send her looks which I intercepted but found inscrutable. I had been looking at her too, watching for her reaction. A boy near me poked another and whispered in mocking awe, "A whole dollar!"

The boy ahead of me jumped suddenly to his feet, banging his leg against the desk so hard that the entire row shook. "Heck," he cried, "we just come from there, too, and I made more'n a buck and a half *every* day." He gave me a triumphant smile and sat down. Then I knew I hated that boy. That night I told my mother about how there was a mean boy just like those other mean boys at the camps and how the teacher *would* have to put me right behind him. "Well," she sighed, " just try not to pay any attention to him."

By the time I had found my sister after school, Barbara and her friends had gone. The next morning when we went to the big house she was gone, too.

After that, my sister and I walked together. Sometimes we would be close enough to hear Barbara's friends, who were always with her, laugh and call her "Bobby." I had never known any Barbaras before, and the name seemed full of unapproachable prestige and sophistication; it was the kind of name that could belong only to a girl who had as many dresses as Barbara Baumann had. "Bobby" was yet more awesome, as if she were as consequential as a boy. At school, if I recited in class, she acted queerly self-conscious, as though she were responsible for me — the way I often felt around my sister when she said something stupid to kids my age.

For various reasons I had that same embarrassed feeling of an enforced distasteful relationship with the boy who sat ahead of me. Once in a while somebody in the class would tease me about him or would say something about "the hop pickers." I was bitterly determined to dissociate myself from the boy, and whenever he turned around to talk to me I would pretend he was trying to copy my paper. I would put my hand over it while I kept my eyes glued to the desk and felt my face grow hot.

There were some things about the school I liked very much. We were allowed to use the library a great deal; and for the first time in my life I had access to numbers of books I hadn't already read. By reading at noon and recess I could finish a book at school every two days. I would also have a book at home that I would read in a couple of nights. One of the nice things about living in a tent was that there were hardly any household chores to do and I could read as much as I wanted.

Frosty mornings came with October, and my sister and I would try to dress under the quilts before we got up to eat our oatmeal. Leaves began to blow across the road, apples grew redder with each cold night, pickers hurried from tree to tree, filling the orchards with the soft thunder of hard round fruit rolling out of picking sacks into boxes, and packers worked faster and faster, trying to get the apples twisted up in fancy tissue and into boxes before they jammed up too thickly on the perpetually moving belts. After school my sister and I would go to the box shed behind the big house where Harry, Barbara's big brother, would be nailing boxes together for a nickel apiece. He was always glad to have company, and would let us stand at a respectful distance and watch him pound in nail after nail with two strokes — a tap to set it, then a mighty clout to send it in — three to an end, six to a side.

One afternoon, with the chill blue sky brilliant behind the orange and black Halloween cutouts on the windows, I was sitting at my desk dreamily drawing a witch in a moon when the teacher called my name. She told me that she wanted me to take all my books out of my desk and take them to the front of the room. Then she told everybody in my row to pack up his books and move one seat back. My heart banged alarmingly up in my throat and I nearly gagged from the sudden acute sensations in my viscera. In North Dakota such drastic action was taken only when an offender, after repeated warnings, had proved too incorrigible to sit anywhere except right in front of the teacher's desk. The fact that I had no idea of why I was now classified as such an incorrigible only augmented my anguish. While books, papers, and pencils fell to the floor and boys jostled each other in the aisle, I managed to sidle numbly up to the front. I sat down in my new seat, trying not to notice how shamefully close it was to the big desk facing it, and I was careful not to raise my eyes higher than the vase of zinnias standing on the corner nearest me.

When school was out I hurried to find my sister and get out of the schoolyard before seeing anybody in my class. But Barbara and her friends had beaten us to the playground entrance and they seemed to be waiting for us. Barbara said, "So now you're in the A class." She sounded impressed.

"What's the A class?" I asked.

Everybody made superior yet faintly envious giggling sounds. "Well, why did you think the teacher moved you to the front of the room, dopey? Didn't you know you were in the C class before, way in the back of the room?"

Of course I hadn't known. The Wenatchee fifth grade

was bigger than my whole school had been in North Dakota, and the idea of subdivisions within a grade had never occurred to me. The subdividing for the first marking period had been done before I came to the school, and I had never, in the six weeks I'd been there, talked to anyone long enough to find out about the A, B, and C classes.

I still could not understand why that had made such a difference to Barbara and her friends. I didn't yet know that it was disgraceful and dirty to be a transient laborer and ridiculous to be from North Dakota. I thought living in a tent was more fun than living in a house. I didn't know that we were gypsies, really (how that thought would have thrilled me then!), and that we were regarded with the suspicion felt by those who plant toward those who do not plant. It didn't occur to me that we were all looked upon as one more of the untrustworthy natural phenomena, drifting here and there like mists or winds, that farmers of certain crops are resentfully forced to rely on. I didn't know that I was the only child who had camped on the Baumanns' land ever to get out of the C class. I did not know that school administrators and civic leaders held conferences to talk about the problem of transient laborers.

I only knew that for two happy days I walked to school with Barbara and her friends, played hopscotch and jump rope with them at recess, and was even invited into the house for some ginger ale – an exotic drink I had never tasted before.

Then we took down our tent and packed it in the trailer with our mattresses and stove and drove on, because the last apples were picked and sorted and boxed and shipped to the people all over the world, whoever they were, who could afford to buy them in 1937. My teacher wrote a letter for me to take to my next school. In it, she told me, she had informed my next teacher that I should be put into the A class immediately. But there wasn't any A class in my room, the new teacher explained.

By then I was traveled enough to realize that it was another special class for transients. The teacher showed us movies almost every day.

Room at the Bottom

IN 1938, when he was twelve and I was eleven, Darius Pfingston and I both understood that the world was passing us by. We looked out from our new, unpainted ship-lap houses perched on the thin mildewed soil of our cut-over hillsides, and we watched the world passing below us on the gravel road and the train tracks and the narrow brown river. On the road went the trucks carrying milk and eggs and vegetables to Seattle, twenty miles west. On the tracks went the boxcars of eggs and iced lettuce to some place thousands of miles east where, hopefully, there was a shortage of eggs and lettuce. Once a day a train went west carrying down from the mountains trees like the ones that had once covered our hills. The butts of them could be twelve feet thick; sometimes there would be only one log to a flatcar. And always there was the little river bringing melted snow and fine soil from the mountains, flowing to the lake which emptied into Puget Sound which emptied into the western ocean.

Every winter as the river passed us by, between its banks of silver willows, under its low simple bridges that looked like the ones in pictures of Holland, through its miles of square green pastures and black fields, beneath its clustered towers of maples and cottonwoods, it rose and spread itself in a gentle foot-deep flood across the bottomland, and it left, like the Nile, the gift of life down there.

Almost every night the river came up to us, too. Slowly the foggy ghost of itself filled the valley. First the mist covered the houses of the people who dwelt in the bottom, then it drifted up around the maples and cottonwoods till only their mighty tops showed in the moonlight like dark castles floating upon a wondrous white kingdom. In the mornings, when the castles had drowned in their kingdom and the fog had passed up our hillside and become the sky, we could no longer see the world passing by, but we could still hear it. If it was summer and the packing shed was working, we would hear the conveyor belts dumping the waste lettuce on a rotting pile. If it was winter, we would hear the school bus honking for Nicky Fuschillo and his cousins.

In summer Darius's mother and mine worked down in the packing shed whenever they were needed. And Darius and I worked in the bottom fields for Nicky Fuschillo's father when there were carrots and lettuce to thin and radishes to pull. By the time we were twelve and eleven, Darius and I had traveled far and done many things in bottom fields, but we had not done nearly so many things nor traveled nearly so far as the braceros, who were brought from two thousand miles away to harvest the peas that were under contract to a chain store.

Our mothers were very much afraid of them — wild men shouting and singing in another language — men long separated from their homes and women. (The saying is that no bracero is ever a father, meaning that no woman north of the Rio Grande can catch a bracero before he slips back across the border.) They camped in the peafields at night and built enormous fires against the foreign fog of the north. Up above, we could smell the smoke in the fog, and if the mist was not too thick, we could see the glow of the fires. And we could hear the savage songs. I don't think the owners of those bottom fields would have got any closer to those fires than my mother would have. For the two weeks of the harvest the bottom belonged to the Mexicans, and so did the night. We would imagine them down there, moving through the glowing mist of the white kingdom. Cards and dice fluttered; knives and teeth flashed; blood and wine gushed from broken vessels; people that nobody ever asked about disappeared forever.

Every year they set the ground on fire. After they had gone, nobody knew where, we would realize that under the thousands of fertile acres, the vast peat stratum was burning. All day and all night the smoke of the burning earth blighted the fresh meadows and fouled the air. Coming from places where a prairie fire was a major catastrophe, Darius and I could never get used to seeing the ground burn and nobody doing anything about it. But those who owned the valley just waited silently for the slow silent rise of the river.

School would start before the fog was again purified of the smoke, and we would hear the bus down the road honking for Nicky. When its yellow lights appeared suddenly in the mist at our stop, Nicky would always be on it. Darius and I did not think that it would have waited for us like that every morning. We were pretty sure that it would have passed us by if we had not been down there ready for it. We were pretty sure that the world was not quite the way people who made movies about it thought it was. Not Hollywood movies. We never saw them. And not the entertainment movies that were shown in the auditorium during the last period of the day once a month. You had to have a dime for those, and so we stayed in the study hall. I mean the movies like *Washington, the Apple State,* or *Yakima Valley, the Cornucopia of the Northwest.* Darius and I would remember all the places in those movies, but we never seemed to remember other things quite the way the Washington Apple Growers or the Yakima Hop Association did. We could not remember our mothers smiling so joyfully in the packinghouses as they snatched up squares of purple tissue paper and twisted the paper quickly around thousands of Premium Red Delicious. We could not remember that our fathers had looked so gallant and successful as they swung the family hop hampers to their shoulders and trudged down the rows to the weighing stations. We did not remember the fields of Blue Lake beans the way the big canning company or the chain store seemed to think they were. And always, in those movies, there were a lot of gay Good Neighbors whose teeth flashed only in sunny rows of tomatoes or in sunny orchards of hops or pears or apricots — never by the light of fires in a chill dark foggy valley. And naturally those Good Neighbors never set the ground to burning for weeks and months.

No, we did not see the world the way other people appeared to see it, and this was only one of the many signs that the world had always gotten along very well without us, and would go on getting along without us. The world even told Darius, wherever he went, that he didn't know how to say his own name. I was in study hall with him that first year in Avondale School when the teacher called his name to check her registration cards. "Der-*eye*-us?" she said. "Der-*eye*-us Pfingston? Is there a Der-*eye*-us in here?

By that point in his life, Darius had been called by the wrong name at least a hundred times, but still, what could he do? Your name was what your parents had named you and what your brothers and sisters called you and what you had always called yourself, wasn't it? So he raised his hand and said, "My name is *Dare*-us."

"Oh?" She looked up from her handful of cards. "But what about the 'i'? I mean, you have three syllables. In fact, Der-*eye*-us is a very famous name. I think I read somewhere it means a rich man."

We had been in that school for only two days, but everybody laughed. So did I. So did Darius. The skin of his face seemed to be made of freckles, but still when he blushed, there were a surprising number of little chinks where the red showed. He was what my mother always called a nice boy, when she worried about the friends I made in the fields and orchards. He never said bad words and he never wanted to go somewhere and play dirty.

I was surprised when I found out how many of the town kids, who had always lived in one place, played dirty under the seats of the grandstand or out in the town park. One thing I had learned in traveling around was that the people who had always lived in one place were better-behaved — at least that was what the world seemed to think. Those of us who came from North Dakota, like me, or from Texas, like Darius, were Okies, and the world seemed to be prepared for almost any kind of crime from us.

That was why we were both so surprised when the bottom world suddenly needed us for something besides doing something to a row of something. It needed us to belong to the Avondale 4–H Garden Club, which was started by Nicky Fuschillo's mother. She came around in the summer to inspect my garden and she helped me arrange my cucumbers and tomatoes on paper plates for the local 4–H fair, which was held in the Avondale school-bus sheds. When the judging was over, Darius and I had blue ribbons taped on every one of our paper plates. It was the first time either of us had made a mark in the world. At the end of the next summer, when he was thirteen and I was twelve, we had more paper plates of vegetables with blue ribbons on them. Also, at the end of that summer, we were about to begin our third year in the same school. The world seemed to be slowing down for us. Or perhaps we were catching up with it. It seemed that we were indeed catching up when Eric Erikson's mother and father decided to start another 4–H club and wanted us to belong to that one, too.

Just after we had moved to Avondale, Darius and I had

climbed to the top of the one virgin fir left on either of our farms, and we had looked across the valley to the Erikson Egg Ranch, with its tiny henhouses and its tinier ranchhouse, and Darius had said, "I guess I'll do that when I grow up. Get me a big ranch." (We believed, like most people nine and ten, that once we were grown up we would do things very differently from the way our parents, who plainly had never caught the world. When we were grown up, we would finally be caught up, too. We would do things right.)

"Only I won't have chickens and chickenhouses on it. I'll have barns and Holsteins – like Carnation Contented Cows." That was a joke with us, about Contented Cows. The cows we knew were calm enough until you tried to get them to do something they didn't want to do – like coming in from new spring pasture when they were nearly dry and didn't care whether they got milked or not.

Certainly neither of us, as we clung to the last fragile branches at the top of the spire that had unaccountably been spared to us half a century before, had had any idea that we would be catching up so fast as to find ourselves, two years later, sitting in the living room of that tiny ranchhouse (which was the biggest house we'd ever seen, when we got inside it), sipping heady drinks of ginger ale, staring into the night through huge French doors, and marveling that people kept plants nine feet high under the ceilings of their living rooms and owned maroon davenports that felt like the fur of the longest-haired kitten you had ever seen.

During the organization part of the meeting, when we were deciding to call ourselves the Avondale 4–H Poultry Club, the County Agent gave us a talk on how the four H's stood for the four petals of a four-leaf clover, and how the four petals, in turn, stood for Head, Heart, Health, and Hands. If a person would put his mind and his soul and his energy and his work into something he believed in, he couldn't help but be successful.

To prove his point the County Agent had brought along one of the outstanding 4–H'ers in the state — a boy whose father was a famous broiler breeder. The boy was going to demonstrate the modern way to slaughter a chicken. We all retired to Mrs. Erikson's gleaming kitchen and the boy strung a line across it from a cupboard-door handle to a light fixture and looped the feet of the chicken in the line so that the bird hung upside down over a pan on the kitchen table.

The chicken waited, beating its wings and salivating over the pan, while the boy explained why a hatchet was obsolete and the curious little knife he held in his hand was the only proper instrument. Then he squeezed the chicken's head till its tongue stood straight out in the middle of its opened beak and he inserted his little knife far back into its throat.

When it had bled enough, he killed it with another stroke through its mouth into its brain, severing, with the same stroke, the nerve that controlled the muscles of the skin. Within two minutes, he had plucked out almost all the feathers without so much as mentioning a scalding bucket. There was no need of a scalding bucket, he pointed out, if one could cut the right nerve, the one that relaxed the skin muscles, and then get the feathers off before rigor mortis set in.

Later, while we had chocolate cake and cocoa, I decided not to go into broiler production, but to stick to eggs for my new 4–H project. Darius decided the same thing, and we both got from the same hatchery a dozen Barred Plymouth Rock sexed females — a dozen dark balls of pedigreed fluff.

Darius used his dozen chicks for his Future Farmers of America project too. That was where he got ahead of me — with the FFA. The world needed him now, not, to be sure, as the star center on the junior high basketball team, or as the president of the eighth grade, or as a rung on the tennis ladder. Nevertheless, it did need him to own a royal-blue jacket with a red-and-white arm badge — to be a member of the national Future Farmers of America. There was no national organization like that for me, to make me believe I belonged — nothing for the Wives of the Future Farmers of America.

Nobody ever gave me a sign like Darius's to hang over the long rutted driveway that led up the hill to my father's acres. Because of the years of misunderstandings about his name, Darius had switched from "Darius Pfingston" to "D. H. Pfingston," and that was what his modest sign said, in two lines of royal-blue letters on a white field, the first line introducing him to the world, as it were:

A FUTURE FARMER OF AMERICA LIVES HERE
D. H. Pfingston

Both of us had wonderful luck with our flocks. After my twelve chickens matured from their erratic pullet ways, I collected ten or eleven eggs every night. It was phenomenal, but my town friends could never understand why. "Doesn't a hen lay an egg every day?" they would say to me. "I thought that was what a hen was for."

I soon gave up trying to explain to them that never in the history of the Council of American Official Poultry Tests had a flock turned in an average like that.

And then, alas, after performing so brilliantly all winter, my flock died, one by one, of some strange plague. So did Darius's. The Eriksons were sympathetic and resigned. Chickens were like that — especially pedigreed chickens. The Eriksons had once lost three thousand chickens from some parasite or fungus or germ that was never identified.

After hygienically cremating the last of our hens, Darius and I became critics instead of producers. We became the hope of the Avondale 4–H Poultry Club hen judging team. At every club meeting we pored over the characteristics of a selected foursome of Erikson White Leghorns and discussed the show ring standards of the laying machine, as Mr. Erikson was fond of calling a hen. He loaned Darius and me all his poultry magazines, which considered such questions as trapnesting, leg banding, mating pens, stud pens, egg filing cabinets, stamping devices to be strapped over the vent for identifying the efficient producers; and the question of oversized eggs vis-a-vis the physiological limitations of the laying machine.

Darius and I memorized flock records, Family Summary Cards, and Breed Qualifications of the National Breeding Plan and of the American Standard of Perfection. At every meeting Mr. Erikson was overjoyed with our progress; from every meeting Mr. Erikson sent us home with new issues of his literature.

I was almost fourteen and Darius was just fifteen when we entered our first judging contest at the county level in late July. Both of us were sensational. Among the four hens in their noisome cage we were offered almost the entire range of laying machines. We showed off everything we knew.

The first hen was in a heavy early molt. We didn't have to take her out of her cage to disqualify her.

The second hen could have been diseased. Darius and I were suspicious of any chicken that would not lift the veil of its eye the instant we touched the latch of its cage. Besides, it lacked the loose, soft depth of abdomen that signified a heavy egg sac full of eggs in all stages of development from the hardshelled AA Extra Large in the egg tube ready for tomorrow morning's devoir down through smaller and smaller yolks to an agglomeration like the roe of fish. Occasionally, my mother would kill a hen she thought had stopped laying only to find a sac full of a month's eggs. Then she would lament her irremediable error all the while she drew the entrails and lungs and heart and gizzard. How, she would ask herself, had she mistaken this faithful layer for that other old biddy she had thought she caught? That one that always tried to hide on the floor any eggs she did lay, and that brooded and clucked and screamed out her determination to be a mother and molted feathers all over the yard.

Well, of course, if my mother had had all my professional training, she would have known that second hen could be no layer.

The third hen, now, could have fooled a lot of people. She had a bright eye, a fine comb, a pair of lusty yellow legs, and a healthy wrath over being dragged from her cage and squeezed and poked and kneaded and provoked into sticking out her horny blade of a tongue. But there was a great deal wrong with her. Her comb was too large and scarlet; she could be the virago that would explode the tensions of a laying house primed for peak production. Her legs and beak and the ring around her eyes were too yellow. If she had been laying, that pigment would have been drained off by the yolks of her eggs. And though she was fat, indeed too fat, her pelvic bones were only an inch apart, indicating that no eggs were traveling through her egg duct. And her abdomen, though heavy, was not loose, but tight and hard — a final damnation.

The fourth hen was everything a laying machine should be. She was thin like a good milch cow, using her food for unselfish production, not lazy fat, and she was not sleek, being too busy laying to spend all day preening. Her shanks, eye ring, beak, and vent were all nearly white. The yellow of them had obviously been going into egg yolks for months. Her abdomen was so deep and full that I could lay three fingers vertically between her pelvic bones, and horizontally between the bottom of her pelvis and her keel. Without resorting to the interior vent investigation that would have confirmed the presence of a hard-shelled egg in her oviduct, I concluded from the heaviness under her tail that she was a layer with a twenty-four-hour interval, and that she might lay every morning for a month before she would skip a day.

I handed down a decision declaring her the perfect White Leghorn hen, supporting my judgment with nearly a page of closely reasoned argument that bristled with verbatim quotations from Mr. Erikson's literature.

That hen proved to be the Grand Champion of the County Fair, as well as of the Erikson flock, and I, in turn, because of the lucidity of my deliberations as well as the precision of my ratings, was hailed by the senior judges of the junior judges to go on, along with the hen, to a State Championship.

Darius did almost as well as I did (he signed his judging sheets "D. H. Pfingston"), and our names appeared in the newspaper story about our club and the Erikson Egg Ranch. The picture with the story showed Eric Erikson squatting in the middle of his winning 4–H project – a flock of one hundred prize hens pedigreed on his father's ranch. The story told about how the Eriksons had demonstrated with Eric's control flock that the livability of chicks and hens could be greatly improved by using red lights instead of regular ones in the brooder pen, pullet range, and layinghouse. The red lights reduced significantly the losses caused by chickens pecking each other to death. White Leghorns, the best layers, are especially prone to killing each other this way because it is so easy for them to see blood on each other. The newest, fuzziest, yellowest, dearest little Easter chicks will peck at red spots until finally the thin-skinned ones are trampled under the exquisite pink toes of the others.

Cannibalism, the Eriksons found in Eric's experiment, was greatly reduced by making all the chicks look red to each other.

Darius and I knew that Mr. Erickson got the idea for Eric's experiment from one of his poultry organs. We also knew that one of the hired men on the ranch had operated Eric's automatic manure remover and fed his chickens for him every night while he stayed in town with Nicky Fuschillo and turned out for the junior varsity football and basketball teams.

(While we went home to our non-automated, non-trapnested hencoops, and, till our hens died, scraped the floors with garden hoes and proudly washed the eleven dirty eggs we found in the outmoded straw-filled laying nests.)

But it would be our turn, we thought, once we got to the State Fair and won the judging championship. Then Darius and I would have our pictures in the paper, too, and not just in the town weekly, but in the Seattle dailies, which always ran pictures of the 4–H owners of Champion and Reserve Champion animals, and also the pictures of the smiling restaurant owners and hotel chefs who had paid three or four dollars a pound for the winning pigs and lambs and steers.

Our whole junior and senior high school went to the State Fair on Students Day because it was educational and free that day. After morning roll was taken, I filed back to the same bus that had brought me to school, feeling for the first time in my life that I was more at home than the town kids. And this bus ride was taking me not to a day of watching my classmates laughing and crying in front of their lockers over the secrets of town girls, and not to a lonely late afternoon of egg washing, henhouse cleaning, or cow catching – but to glory.

Mr. and Mrs. Erikson had both said so. The town kids were going to the fair to spend their fantastic allowances (even the idea of an allowance was fantastic to me) on the froth that was meant to be only a refreshing accompaniment to the work and progress represented at a fair. They knew nothing of the justification, the purpose of a fair. For once it would be they, not I, who did not understand; they who belonged on the edge, not in the center.

Darius and I and the other two members of our team waited under the portals of a building which was painted with block letters five feet high: POULTRY. It was not only the lettering on this building that was five times bigger than it had been at the County Fair. So was the noise five times as loud. So was the smell five times as strong.

When the Eriksons finally arrived to register us, Eric was not with them. He was going to visit the Poultry Building later, Mrs. Erikson explained. Meanwhile, Mr. Erikson chuckled, Eric was last seen hanging upside down from the Octopus in a glass coop.

Somebody with an armband led us off to eight rows of cages — one row of hens and one row of pullets for each team member. In each row were four cages, and in each cage was a dirty, skinny White Leghorn hen. She was nearly dead from the heat, her eyes were dull and veiled, her comb and legs and vent were pallid, her abdomen was noncommittal, her attitude was that of a chicken on the verge of dying from a mysterious plague. Until I took hold of her legs.

Then she became the incarnation of the hatred all laying machines feel for all members of chicken judging teams. Again and again I lifted out each flapping squawking hen. I shut my eyes, waiting for some skipped-over page of Mr. Erikson's literature to come back to me. When the page didn't come back, I kept my eyes shut till I was sure that when I opened them again, the chickens would all look different — that one would have a deformed beak, another a grossly crooked breastbone that I had somehow missed seeing.

When I opened my eyes, the only thing that looked different were the places where my three teammates had been standing. They were all gone — even Darius.

Finally I submitted, on the imposing but cramped State Fair judging blanks, my rating of the four hens and four pullets. There was hardly any space for Remarks, the space in which I had distinguished myself at the County Fair.

After turning in my sheets, I wandered toward the grandstand where the livestock was being judged. I thought I might find Darius around there, because it was Holsteins he really cared about. Besides, this was the show ring I had always loved. Here the animals did not peck you and make you jump idiotically, the way you jumped when you carelessly brushed against your father's electric fence while you were buried to the ankles in an upland swamp. Here in this ring there were no ignominious shocks, no ridiculous threats. Here, if you didn't know exactly how to handle the ring in his nose, the Grand Champion Holstein bull, his hundred-thousand-dollar organ haughtily displayed before his knees, would hook you with a horn and finish you with a twenty-five-hundred-pound hoofprint. Or the Grand Champion Clydesdale stallion would take a six-inch bite out of your ribs and kick you into the twelfth row of spectators.

How silly chickens were! For days after they were hatched, you couldn't even tell whether they were male or female unless you were a high-paid professional Japanese sexer who had brought his secrets over from Japan.

When I didn't see Darius in any of the royal-blue knots of FFA boys around the judging ring or in the Bovine or the Equine building, I knew that he understood he wasn't going to buy a prize heifer and start a prize dairy. He knew he wasn't going to be a Future Farmer of America. He was just going to work for one.

Meanwhile, he would be out on the midway, linking his royal-blue elbow with the blue elbows of ten other Future Farmers of America, who also understood that there was not going to be any more cheap pastureland waiting for something so common as an eagerness to use Head, Heart, Health, and Hands to get ahead. It was easy to see why there were so many blue knots enjoying the froth with the town kids and so few blue knots in the exhibition buildings and judging rings.

I went through the Produce building on my way to the carnival and I saw a marvelous sun either rising or setting from the railing at my waist to the flag-draped beams of the ceiling forty feet above me. The sun was a ten-foot half-circle of prize tomatoes turned bottoms out. Rays of prize tomatoes streaked across a concentric spectrum of carrots, zucchini, cabbage, and eggplant. From the orange horizon to the purple zenith it was a sunrise, or sunset, of consequence.

The sign beneath the sunrise or sunset read FUSCHILLO BROS. KING COUNTY. That sun made me understand about Nicky Fuschillo – about the glorious screeching of his name that went up when we arrived late at a basketball game. It was a cry that placed him in the world, pulled him along the black boundary lines of the gymnasium, past the out-of-bounds bodies, the glistening skin and long shivering muscles of the seniors racing over the court and slamming against the tumbling mats hung on the walls behind the baskets. That cry guided Nicky around the bouncing bodies, through the sweating overheated air, and up the packed bleachers to a squeezed saved place between two town kids. "Yea, *Nick-eee!*"

In the Equine building the people came to look at Belgians and Percherons as they would have come to see dinosaurs and mammoths. Horses were not part of the world any more, except for the amusement of city people who could afford to own country land. Cows and chickens were not really part of the world any more, either. It was, of course, true that the Bovine building housed the champion sires of the world's finest U.S. Choice T-bone steaks. And the Poultry building caged the world's greatest laying machines of Grade AA Extra-Large ova. But the Bovines and Poultry did not really matter any more to most of the people who mattered. Even the smaller Equines mattered more than the Bovines or Poultry. For the Equines there were at least the suburban gymkhanas starring girls my age who wore dental braces and high-priced jodhpurs. But that particular kind of intimacy with the animals still surviving in the world was hardly relevant to me: there were no blooded saddle horses on my father's rented stump farm.

"Student Day at the State Fair was very educational," I could begin my Fair theme to be required the next day in English class. But even if I could have successfully explained what I had just come to understand, the teacher would have disapproved. I understood, first of all, that it wasn't just a question of catching up with the world, the way they would tell Darius and me when we went from one school to another and never seemed to fit in any grade. No, once you caught up with the world, you still had to find a place on it. Like Nicky Fuschillo coming in the gym when all the seats were gone and even the town businessmen were standing in their overcoats back in the shadowy corners behind the bleachers, shivering in the freezing draft from the emergency exits – like Nicky Fuschillo zigzagging to the top of the bleachers, stepping on coats and scarves and fingers, and squeezing into a saved seat.

Once I had believed what everybody told me: that there was always room at the top. (Nobody had told me that there was always room at the bottom: people don't say things like that to children.) But now I understood that the room at the top had disappeared along with the good bottomland.

I headed back to the bus. I walked through the long oval shadow of the revolving Ferris wheel and watched the shadows of the people on it waving across my own shadow. When I climbed up the high steps of the bus, I saw Darius in the rear corner that the blue-jackets had saved for themselves. He was always in that blue corner now; it seemed as though every time I passed a study hall window I would see him back there with the other Future Farmers of America, quietly doing nothing.

They thought they would make a place for themselves

at the bottom, those blue-jackets, by sticking together and saving seats for each other. I couldn't understand why I had ever been puzzled because Nicky Fuschillo and Eric Erikson did not join the FFA. Darius's little white sign looked just right over his rutted hillside driveway, but that sign would have been egregious in front of the Fuschillo packing shed where Darius's mother and mine sorted lettuce. And I couldn't even imagine that sign hung between the two twelve-foot statues of White Leghorn hens that flanked the white gravel approach to the Erikson Egg Ranch.

The bus driver had started the engine when Mrs. Erikson rushed up and stopped him by planting her high-heeled foot on the heavy iron step. She paged me in an embarrassed way, and after I had worked my way up the aisle to her, she handed me a yellow rosette with some gold lettering lost in the satin. She explained that this fourth-place ribbon for my chicken judging was far more important than all my first-place ribbons won at the County Fair.

Mrs. Erikson had done all she could. She had made efforts, been one of the smiling people in charge who gave out blue ribbons, blue jackets, badges, club memberships, cocoa, chocolate cake, signs — one of those people who had spared us the truth about the room at the top as long as they could. I understood that she felt guilty about us and that was why she had put up with all of us sitting around her living room every week, running our hands against the fur of her maroon davenport. By the time she let me go, I was much more embarrassed than she was, because I was beginning to understand what an embarrassment I was to the world.

I got home in time to feed and water the chickens and wash the dirty eggs laid in old fashioned straw nests. As I walked down the hill from our ship-lap chickenhouse to our ship-lap farmhouse, the mist from the river rose to meet me. Down in the valley the Mexicans were cooking their supper in the fog. I know now that they understood something I still did not understand. I still believed that no matter who owned the bottom, there would always be plenty of room for people who needed to work down there.

But those braceros had traveled many years and many miles to find their kind of room at the bottom. They knew, hidden away under the fog kingdom, with their flashing knives and their flashing teeth, that just because you were willing to exchange your Head, Heart, Health, and Hands for a place at the bottom, you wouldn't necessarily find one.

Maybe that was why, gaily every August, those singing Mexicans set the earth on fire.

❦❦❦❦ Epitaph for a Lion

Until I went away to college, I lived on my parents' farm set in the slopes of a little valley named for its river, the Sammamish, about fifteen miles due east of Seattle. In winter the river would rise and spread a foot of water upon the flat acres below us, and when the water froze we would ice-skate over rows of cabbage stalks left standing after the harvest. In summer the river provided irrigation for the prosperous truck farmers who sold their produce in the city. The bottomland and the first low hills slanting away from it offered enough room for the valley's inhabitants so that the steep upper hills were left to the jungle that took possession of them after they had been stripped of their virgin forests. They were covered with twisted vine-maple, weedy alders, acres of salmon-berry brambles, yellow-green ferns seven or eight feet high, and clumps of Devil's Clubs — a combination of tree and vine which towered wickedly over the brush, the dark-brown stems covered with gigantic thorns and the curling arms brandishing thistled leaves twice the size of a human head. Patches of second growth fir, tall and dense enough to shade out the writhing confusion about them, furnished the only respite from chaos. In swamps lying between the ridges, streams trickled their beginnings around hummocks blooming with skunk cabbages and then flowed down through the fields to the river.

The five hills on our farm ramble west and finally merge into a rumpled highland that descends into the waters of Lake Washington. It is a famous lake now because hydroplane races are held there. Fifteen or twenty years ago it was not so famous, but one could ride across it for a dime on a fine old ferryboat called the *Leschi*, which was replaced twelve years ago by an older, smaller, slower boat called the *Duwamish*, which was replaced eight years ago by a bridge. Other hills rise again from the west side of the lake, but they are all covered with Seattle, which seemed far away when my sisters and I were little.

At any rate it was far enough away so that animals like coyotes and wildcats, which Seattlites went to the zoo to see, roamed wild in the hills on our side of the lake, hunting the rabbits, gophers, squirrels, quail, and mountain beaver that abounded there. Sometimes in the spring, when the stupefied black bears came yawning and starving out of their long buried sleep in the mountains, one of them would stray down to our valley in search of food and manage to involve himself in some foolish encounter with humans. I remember one bleary fellow who was grubbing in the tall grass along a hedgerow separating one field from another when a young fieldhand came driving a cat tractor toward him, with its revolving treads tossing chunks of matted earth into the air and its vitals emitting a thunderous challenge. The panicky bear shot up out of the grass on his hind legs, and the tractor driver, like a crazed soldier deserting a tank for a battlefield, leaped from his seat and ran, leaving a twelve-thousand-dollar machine to wander aimlessly along an eight-foot irrigation ditch. The owner of the tractor was not amused, but most of the rest of us were delighted, not just with the story but with the idea that wilderness could still discomfit civilization.

That civilization remained unchanged for many years. Two or three new houses went up — one of them built by a furniture dealer from Seattle who named his five acres The Fancy-Free Ranch, and then opened a store in the little town at the end of the valley. People snickered over the sign at the driveway to his ranch and went on harvesting flowers, fruit, and vegetables and carting them off to the markets in Seattle. Tank trucks filled with milk continued to bump along the casual gravel road, headed for the creameries across the lake.

Then one morning a legend came to inhabit the valley. One of the boys on our school bus told us that the night before a lion had killed and dragged away one of his father's goats. What was his proof? Blood, a missing goat, and in the goat pen a great cat track. We were skeptical, not because we didn't want to believe him but because we wanted so much to believe him.

I was fourteen then, and I didn't want a ten-year-old to think he could impress me, but I began planning how I would cut up through our woods that night after school to get a look at that track. It was four or five miles to his place by road, but not more than two miles straight over our hills. I would take my Ernest Thompson Seton book with the drawings of tracks, to make the identification positive. But as the morning wore on, I began picturing the thing that might be hiding in those woods where twenty head of cattle could lose themselves. I felt sheepishly relieved when I heard rain strike the school building and realized there would be no track to investigate. I wondered if there really could be a beast out there in the rain — his stomach full of bad-smelling goat, hair and all, backed in under a roof of brush, his yellow eyes closed in sleep and his black-lipped muzzle resting on two practiced paws.

By the time I got home that night I wasn't even the first to bring the news; my father had heard about it when he was in town getting a haircut. He was skeptical too, until a few days later when the cougar got a late-fall calf not far from the scene of its first kill. This time the game warden went out to look and discovered what he said were the tracks of an exceptionally large lion — an old one, he decided, who couldn't run down a deer any more, and had strayed down from the mountains to find easier hunting.

Even after we began to hear him scream in the night, sounding horribly like a woman being murdered, some of us couldn't really believe in him. It was incredible that such an elemental enemy should range across the land that had long been so neatly and legally ruled off in acres and sections and water rights. The ordered miles of cabbages and lettuce we looked down on from our living-room windows scoffed at the idea of a mountain lion at our backs.

Perhaps to make sure that he really did exist, my father wanted to organize a hunt to get him, but the lion was a wary old transient, and not enough men were willing to take part in what might well be a fruitless expedition — not even those few who had lost a calf or a goat. Indeed, those whose animals had been eaten were in a kind of aristocracy. They participated in the larger, more fundamental issues of the world. If, after all, the cougar didn't exist, maybe they didn't want to know. And if he did — a legend for a valley was better than a cougar skin in a farmhouse. I can't help thinking that was the way they felt, whether they knew it themselves or not.

After a few months I began to have some complex feelings about that lion. In the middle of the night I might wake in a cold sweat to the sound of his screams, but after the first shock of terror had been dispelled by the rationality of complete wakefulness, I would lie in bed feeling so grateful that it was only the cougar screaming. The war was less than a year old then, and we were living in partial blackout, wondering if the radio would fall silent and we would hear the echoes of Japanese bombs crumbling Seattle into Puget Sound. There was little that ordinary people could do, besides conscientiously adjusting their blackout blinds and memorizing the instructions for what to do if an incendiary bomb hit the house.

(Never use a hose. Incendiary bombs are too hot to be extinguished by water and a stream of water will only spread the fire. Douse with sand.) I read those instructions posted all over the school, the church, the post office, and the community center where the Girl Scouts met, and I always wondered how you could get close enough to something that hot to douse sand on it, assuming that you were holding a bucket of sand when the bomb came through the ceiling. The thing about the lion was that he presented a threat which could be dealt with rationally. We had only to stay out of the hills and we would be safe.

Of course there were disadvantages in not being able to trust the woods. My sisters and I couldn't go alone to saw down the Christmas tree and bring it back in independent triumph. We went with my father, who carried his gun. When summer came, we knew there were whole hillsides laced with vines of delicate wild blackberries, but we couldn't go to pick them. Most of all I missed using some of my favorite thinking places.

As usual, the cow managed to hide her newborn calf somewhere in the five hills and we had some anxious hours after she came down to feed at the barn until she felt moved to wander back to him and we could follow her. That time it seemed that the big cat must be very near indeed; he, too, must be stalking the lonely baby, and if we managed to find it first, he would be poised somewhere over us when we finally bent to nudge it to its feet and coax it back to safety. It must have been my first sight of that calf's tottering vulnerability which makes me still so sure that I was hunted that day.

For nearly a year our valley was included in the lion's wide foraging range. We wouldn't hear him or hear of any killing for weeks at a time, but just when I was getting resigned to relegating him entirely to legend, he would return again, and life seemed somehow simpler. No bombs or other nightmares exploited the helpless night; only the cougar screamed in the blackness of the hills.

One late afternoon when my father and mother were in town grocery shopping, I was out hauling wood with my five-year-old sister while the cold dusk of an autumn night settled about us. A scream not three hundred yards behind us exploded into the valley, and then a second contended with the echo of the first, and another and another, capturing my heart and breath in the rhythm of fury. My paralysis was broken by the maniacal barking of dogs, and I realized that they had treed him. The classic hatred of cat for dog and dog for cat blown into such massive scale was suddenly deliriously funny, and I stood there in the cold with my arms full of wood, laughing while my little sister cried and begged me to take her into the house. I told her to go by herself – it was not fifty feet away – but she wouldn't let go of my jacket.

The lion was at the very edge of the woods where we stopped farming and let the jungle take over. He was close to the corner of the pigpen, and he must have been really hungry to be hunting at that time of day. The dogs from the entire valley began arriving for the fight, and judging by the noise they made, the dogs from two or three other valleys must have been there too. They came yelping across our yard, shedding civilization with every bound, their jaws foamy and their tongues stretched out purple just from the effort of getting to the scene of action.

The cougar had never been anywhere nearly so close to us before, nor had he ever made a sound in daylight. Now I knew, once and for all, that he was real, and I knew that all my life that certainty would make a difference.

When my parents drove into the yard my father jumped from the car, having heard the racket far down the road. He said, just the way he would have in a comic movie about hillbillies, "Get my gun!"

"John!" my mother shrieked. "You *can't* go up there in

this light! You *know* you can't see well enough to hit anything. The dogs have got him so wild that he's liable to spring right out of the tree on you. You wouldn't have a chance. You *can't* go!"

My father probably saw her logic, though he later claimed he didn't go just because of "the women's hysterics." He grumbled a good deal and seemed very envious of the dogs.

After it had been dark a long time, the screams stopped. There was no sign of a dead cougar the next morning, so he must have either waited out all the dogs, or somehow given them the slip. I suppose that as the dogs lost their voices they began regaining their sanity and thinking of overdue dinners. We could hear them come slinking back through our yard, pausing to throw back hoarse insults over their shoulders, and then panting home to recuperate from their heroism.

As far as I know, nobody ever got himself a bounty and a rug. The cougar either died of old age or retired to another valley for good. I don't think we ever heard him again, and in a few weeks the woods were deemed safe once more. But I was just past fifteen by then, and whenever I went to one of my favorite thinking spots, like the somber little fir forest in a far corner of our property, I found myself doing nothing but worrying about boys, and I felt nostalgic for the simple dangerous days that had been.

Now with my husband and two small children I go home to that valley in the summer to escape the smog where we live. The valley is filling up with "ranchhouses" owned by people who commute over the bridge to Seattle. They all hang out signs by their driveways like the one the furniture dealer has, so that their city friends will have no trouble in finding Pine Tree Cottage or Lazy Acres. (The trees are firs, the cottage has eight rooms with two and a half baths, and the farmers can't see that it's the overgrown acres that are lazy.) The little gravel road has been modernized with asphalt and occasionally a fine free collie who overestimated his freedom lies stiff and bloody beside it. Another pontoon bridge will soon float another four-lane highway across the brisk waves of Lake Washington, and businessmen in our little town rub their hands when they think about it.

From our porch I look down at the lake of evening mist drifting over the river and wonder when it will begin to take on the brown tinge I know so well, and when it will burn to brown the rich green of the cabbage stalks I used to skate over. It is twenty-two years since the cougar left us, and I wonder, if he came back again, if his commanding presence could blot out missiles and fallout and lung cancer, and give us something reasonable to fear.

But I know there will never be another lion here, because taxes have made wilderness too expensive. My father is going to sell our five jungled hills to a developer of "view lots" overlooking each other down concrete terraces, where perhaps for a few years a stubborn Devil's Club root will burst through and crack a cement wall.

I hope that lion went back home to die. His bones should never sleep beneath a barbecue or a carport.

The Loop in Time

. . . because everything is irrevocable,
Because the past is irremediable,
Because the future can only be built
Upon the real past.

. . . .

The man who returns will have to meet
The boy who left. Round by the stables,
In the coach-house, in the orchard,
In the plantation, down the corridor
That led to the nursery, round the corner
Of the new wing, he will have to face him—
And it will not be a very jolly *corner.*
When the loop in time comes—and it does not
come for everybody—
The hidden is revealed, and the spectres show themselves.

—T. S. Eliot
The Family Reunion

TO MY GRANDMOTHERS
Margaret Anne Runner
1881–1960
Floradel Phillips
1879–

IN THE BEGINNING the first snow falls on the prairie: snow filters between the brown rotted stalks of frozen stubble, then snow calks the unending seams of summer-fallowed earth, then snow slips through the barbed wire, fills the wide, deep, straight ditches, spills across the falling fans of lath fences; snow wraps softly the wheel of the world and stops the wheel of the merry-go-round. It will not stop falling, even though all the children inside the schoolhouse are willing it to stop until the recess bell rings, for fear there will not be any left to fall on them when their minutes of liberty come.

It still falls as they, rejoicing, slide down the steps in haste to make their marks of uniqueness. They make angels, lying on their backs and sweeping robes and wings and halos with their overshoes and mittens and the tiny round backs of their stocking caps, while the snow pats down on their mouths and noses and eyelids. They think it is pretending not to know they are there, pretending they are only part of the ground. They leap and kick and flounder and gouge, in order to make bruises in the snow that are their own.

Then one begins the circle — they call it a pie — and all follow, happy to be only feet weighted with boots and thick underwear and wet winter clothes: just feet following and followed by other feet making a narrow blue round ditch. Now comes the moment when the prairie is conquered; the wobbly loop meets its beginning with its end, the first set of boots returns to the first track it made and, followed by the obedient chain, cuts the pie in two, then cuts it again and again, until there are many pieces and corners, and nobody knows any more — not even he who began and closed the circle — where the last boot track met the first.

They are all concerned now, for a moment, with the corners, with the game, with escaping if they are the geese, and with capturing if they are the fox. But it has taken them such a long time to make the pie and to cut it and to stamp out the little blue circle of safety in the center. They have scarcely begun the game, they think, when the recess bell rings. There was so much more space than there was time.

Every recess they forget about this imbalance. All children, while they make their ears deaf and their elbows numb on their arithmetic books, while they watch the snow and wait for recess — all children forget about this one imbalance. They believe that if there is space enough, there will also be time enough.

There will be time enough to discover, if they care to, the place where the loop meets — the secret of the circle. There will be time enough to understand, time enough to meet themselves, time enough to prove that they are unique, that they could not have occurred at any other juncture, at any other ringing of the bell.

The circle seems small enough when you yourself are so small you cannot cross the street without holding your mother's hand. Then you tug at her glove and point your finger and ask loud questions and she silences you by promising that soon, perhaps that very day when you get home, you will be told the answers to your questions. You will understand the secrets of the people who have tramped out the circle ahead of you, and so you will understand the circle.

It is the old people who have gone farthest ahead, and so they have the most secrets, and the most important secrets.

It is the grandmothers who keep the secrets that prove we are not accidents but unique in the universe. They are the real past, upon which the only real future can be built. The grandmothers shade their foreheads with flat hands in a salute to some distant grandness we cannot see. When we first come to know them, we believe they are the set of boots that made the first track, the set that will close the circle.

When I was three years old, my father's widowed mother was keeping house for an ancient man who ate his peas with his knife. "Does Mr. Bangs eat his peas with his knife because he doesn't have any teeth?" I would ask her.

I wanted to understand my real past. I wanted to understand the secrets of the old people.

"*Ssshhh!*" my father's mother would say. "Mr. Bangs thinks that's the way to eat them. Now be *quiet*."

Obviously Mr. Bangs had not hit upon the most efficient way of eating peas. His hand shook and most of the peas he managed to float upon his knife blade trembled off long before he got them to his fluttering lips, which, in turn, dislodged all but one or two of the survivors. Why *did* Mr. Bangs choose to eat his peas with his knife? His secret seemed to be part of the secret of my grandmother, since my grandmother would not tell it to me.

This was my mountain grandmother, transplanted from Tennessee to the North Dakota prairie, and though you would say that she was a prairie woman, still she was always different from the rest of us. Her transplanting never faded or wilted her; she became a green and gold and purple flower, as surprising and as familiar as the crocuses that appear, mysteriously and regularly, around the same rock on the same hillside in the same part of every spring. She did not wilt — as crocuses do not wilt, but only appear and disappear — but she was not proud, either, in the way of my mother's mother.

My mother's mother wore prairie colors, not flower colors,

and she was the proudest human being I have ever known. All her life she fought the sin of pride. In all the time I knew her, there was never any gap that I could see between what she believed and what she did. And yet she cried over small things that seemed to have no relevance to the great, rigid, noble pattern of her life. She could not bear the small lapses, the tiny departures that nobody else could even see.

She could see everything; at least when I was small I thought she could. All prairie people, like desert people, can recognize from a great distance the elongated dots of their kind. They know, when a speck appears on the unchanging rim of the world, whether or not it is human. It was as though my grandmother viewed, from some spot high in the air, the whole circle of the earth and could see all the dots moving on it and knew what each dot ought to be doing. My mother's mother, though she required most of herself, required also a great deal of all other human dots — especially me. But since her requirements appeared to be based on her knowledge, they seemed justified, if stern.

For sixty-five years her green eyes looked out across the world and saw only the dots and what they ought to be doing — saw no reasons and no excuses. Then one day, with those far-seeing eyes, she began to read Freud.

What made her decide, after sixty-five years, that it was questions, not answers, the world was full of? If I should ever happen upon the answer to this question, perhaps I would understand some of her other secrets. But all I know is that while I was in college she read Freud, and then his followers. I was the one who got her most of the books she wanted, and I think I was the only person she talked to about what she read.

Not that she ever said much. I would be home for a weekend or on vacation and we would find ourselves briefly alone — finishing the supper dishes, shelling peas, working on the Sunday crossword puzzle — and she would say, while the peapods went pop under her thumb or the scalding water hissed against the plates, "If I'd only known forty years ago what I know now," or "Do you really think all little girls go through a castration complex stage?"

Of all the things she read about in Freud, the female resentment of the male must have been the most vivid and convincing to her. In fact, she would not have asked me that question if she had not been remembering how much she had wanted to be a boy. Boys did not have to wear skirts to their ankles, boys got bicycles and educations, boys grew up to be the only people who mattered in the world. Why did she ask her question as though she hoped I would say that Freud was mistaken?

The questions do not come in any kind of order, nor do the answers. You turn one corner and find the question you asked yesterday. You turn another corner and discover an answer that once fit a question you forgot long ago.

Why did my father's mother, who never heard of Freud, decide, in her late sixties, after nearly thirty years of sensible widowhood, to marry a white-haired, yellow-toothed prospector?

She met him at Svenska Hall. Between the barber shop and The Alibi was a dark narrow cave set back from the sidewalk. A flight of sinister stairs proceeded from the cave to a landing from which a door opened into Svenska Hall. Over the landing was a black sign with peeling gold letters, suspended from chains. On Thursday and Saturday nights a forty-watt bulb was turned on above the sign, and all the moral people passing below on the sidewalk could look up and read it: SVENSKA HALL.

One night when I was fifteen years old and I was walking home with two of my friends after Thursday choir practice, I watched my grandmother's prospector come out of The Alibi, keeping his back against the wall, and slide up the stairs sideways, still with his back pressed against the wall, till he slid through the door of Svenska Hall. One had only to walk through that door to be in the world where everybody knew everything that nobody is supposed to know, and consequently had so much fun. Anyway, that was what my friends and I thought at the time. They had so much fun up there that the town reverberated, from week to week, with the news of whose black-sheep cousin had picked a fight with whose black-sheep brother and which of them had been pitched down the stairs by the other.

No matter what the season, no matter what the needs of Svenska Hall for ventilation, red brothel curtains tightly covered all its windows. But when a dance was going on, the door was always open, and a person standing on the sidewalk could look up the stairs and see the thumping legs of the initiated and the damned. I don't know how many years my grandmother had been going there to dance, because it wasn't till I was fifteen that it mattered to me.

These two friends of mine, my best friends, walked me past Svenska Hall every Thursday night after choir practice, and every Thursday night they wanted to sneak up the stairs and watch through the door to see if they could catch a couple of people from our class who had gone wild, and every Thursday night I knew my grandmother would be up there flinging herself around with any man on the floor who was sober enough to keep up with her.

I can't remember, any more, how I managed, week after week, to argue my friends out of spying on Svenska Hall. I remember only that I was always successful, that I lived for about a year in a long nightmare in which I was either arguing successfully or desperately concocting the next argument, and that if I had ever lost an argument I would have run away from home, like a girl in our class who had got herself pregnant.

This mountain grandmother of mine, my father's mother,

never fit any pattern that any of the rest of us could recognize. That must have been one reason why she had such a good time at Svenska Hall. Almost everybody else up there had to be drunk in order to believe that the world was simple enough so that a human being could be happy. But my grandmother was always perfectly sober. She just went up those stairs and enjoyed herself. And on Sunday mornings, there she was in church, listening to me sing in the choir, wearing a shiny green dress she had made herself, and large shiny purple earrings and purple beads, and picking me out in the choir to smile at with her polished store teeth — the only person in the congregation who had danced in Svenska Hall until it closed earlier that morning.

The loop in time seems, these few years later, like a knot around my throat when I think of those Thursday nights when I suffered so many foolish agonies. If only my grandmother were still dancing up in Svenska Hall, I would drag all my friends up the dirty wooden stairs and push them through the sweating crowd at the door and make them watch her laughing and flinging herself about with her white-haired prospector.

My father's mother and my mother's mother: they both had green eyes and brown hair and they were both mostly Celtic (Irish, Scotch, and Welsh) and the rest English. Otherwise, they were utterly unlike each other. Why was it, then, that each of them thought I was just like her? What things did they remember about themselves that I reminded them of — things they never could or never would tell me? I look like my mother's mother, who was thin of nose and spare of rib, but for many years, while I got thinner and thinner, my father's mother would say, "She's going to take after me. I can see it. She's getting fleshy, like me." And my mother's mother would say, "You're drinking too much coffee. It will make you have a brown skin, like mine. You must try not to get the habit. You're too much like me." And her eyelids would redden and she would turn away. The tears were waiting to come, the tears over a weakness.

Because of my long sorrows over bicycles I once found out one of the old secrets of my mother's mother. A town friend of mine in the sixth grade was stealing her big brother's bicycle on Saturday mornings and riding out to our farm and trying to teach me to ride on the rutted gravel road that ran the length of our valley. Bessie, my friend, belonged to a large family that had migrated from Missouri about the time my family had migrated from North Dakota. In 1936 we were not welcome on the Pacific Coast; we were all Okies. If we had not been outcasts together, we probably would not have been friends. Bessie's brother Garald was one of those tall, speechless boys who disappear from school on the day they are legally old enough to go free and then disappear in the world—into some sweltering oily place or some sweltering dusty place where we see them every day, all the while wondering where they have gone.

Because of Garald's appalling machine and Bessie's boundless patience and my grandmother's astounding erudition, I finally learned to ride a bicycle. Now when I ride my English racer, I think of them all. Week after week Bessie sneaked away with the one wheeled possession of her family and rode it out to me. Then she gave me all the strength of her long skinny limbs, running up and down the gravel road beside me, saving me from falling into the deep ditch of stagnant water on one side or the foamy green swamp on the other.

Week after week I made no progress. At some moment long before Bessie's brother acquired the bicycle, its seat had permanently rusted itself to the frame in a position that was about three inches too high for me. I could never get a proper start. Hoping that I would not split myself in two, I would throw myself over the bike without ever catching my balance and wobble through the treacherous gravel, never able to trust myself without Bessie there steadying the handlebars.

Finally we would go up to the house for lunch, where we sat flushed and weak, as glum and professional over our food as threshers. Then Bessie would hurry home before Garald discovered that his bicycle was missing. It never occurred to me that my grandmother was aware of what went on down there on the road, a quarter of a mile below our cherry orchard. But one day she said to me, "Aren't you supposed to turn your handlebars the same way you're falling? Isn't that the way you balance a bicycle? Isn't that the principle?"

I tried her principle the next Saturday and learned to ride a bicycle. At the end of that triumphant session, I asked my grandmother how she had come to know such a useful principle, since she did not know how to ride a bicycle.

"I read a book on it once," she said.

I never asked her the name of the book. My question was answered. From that moment on I was interested only in the question of how I could manage to own a bicycle. I memorized the specifications of every bicycle in every catalogue issued for every season by Sears, Roebuck and Montgomery Ward. I knew how many ball bearings were in every pedal, how many plies were in every tire, how deluxe were the grips, how pure was the chrome plate.

I was picking things to earn a bicycle. I picked beans, peas, raspberries, strawberries, cherries, apples, blackberries. For hundreds of nights I went to bed too tired to sleep, seeing somewhere in my brain the rows and vines and branches of the things I was picking. I saw myself filling boxes, flats, carriers, pails, hampers. I saw myself filling the tickets in my dirty pants pocket with punches, and I saw myself turning in the tickets for checks and turning in the checks for a bicycle — only the last bit of the vision never came true.

I see now that my mother's mother, having been recently widowed and having lost the North Dakota farm she and my grandfather spent their lifetime building, might have felt some despair of her own, but at the time my own despair was too great for me to be aware of anybody else's. She and I were out in her sweetpea patch one day when I had begun to give up on the triumphant culmination of my vision — the proud wheels flashing, the spokes twinkling, as I in my independence rolled the new bicycle out for its maiden cruise. I had been laid off from my strawberry picking until the berries were ripe again, and I was picking sweetpeas *gratis* for my grandmother. She was not raising sweetpeas because, like other grandmothers, she thought they were pretty. She was raising them to sell to Seattle florists. I was cutting the longest stems I could, gooey to the elbow from the dust and spray on the leaves and the milk flowing in the vines, and I was looking for a yellow sweetpea.

My grandmother had read in a book that a pure yellow sweetpea which would yield seeds that would produce yellow sweetpeas would be worth from ten to twenty thousand dollars. My grandmother was positive that she would discover the pure yellow sweetpea. What I did not understand then was that she was so proud she believed it was possible for a human being to justify his existence.

She was going to justify her existence not only by ceasing to "live off" us, but also by making us all solvent. So there we both were in our own rows of despair, seeking the yellow sweetpea that would be our justification, when she came snipping her way abreast of me and said, "You know, when I was about your age, I wanted a bicycle so bad I tried to make myself one out of hay wire and old mowing machine wheels."

The idea of a bicycle made of baling wire and iron wheels six inches wide was not nearly so startling as the idea that my grandmother had ever *wanted* anything in the way that I wanted something.

That was the first and almost the only time she ever spoke to me about a part of her life when she was the same age as I, but from then on I sensed the confrontations and the repetitions of the generations. I could see her on the farm of her father, who sometimes whipped her with a buggy whip. She would be at the foot of a long hill, tugging the iron wheels from buffalo grass that came nearly to her shoulder, untangling the spokes from the whitened stems they had crushed away from the sun. She would look guiltily about in all directions, then she would set swiftly to work with her pliers. I could feel the beating of her heart as she mounted her bicycle. I could feel the bruises as the naked steel seat of an old reaper collapsed over the wires and the monstrous wheels rolled back into the grass, and I could feel the ache in her throat as she cried to herself about how foolish she had been and went crawling after the pliers. How many times did she build it before she gave up?

My grandmother could not make me happier; she could not buy me a bicycle. But she made me see how much peoples' lives are alike. If there is not a catalogue automatically falling open at the bicycle pages every time it is picked up, there is something else to break the hearts of one generation or another. Our mightiest strivings may bring us only to a suddenly painful corner, a corner we seem to recognize with our own anguish, even if it is a place where only our grandmothers have been before.

Once when I asked her how old she was, my mother's mother told me that she was born in the one year which could be read upside down or backwards and still be the same. Finally I had to give up and let her tell me the answer — 1881. She was just the right age when the first bicycling craze came, but not even my mother knew how that craze had mattered to her. I was the one to whom she confessed the secret that generations cannot bear to confess to each other — that they are all alike. That they all care the most about the things that they tell themselves matter the least. It was by chance, because one day we were both looking for the yellow sweetpea, that she told me the secret that has made me imagine a thousand other secrets. And so far as I know, nobody has yet discovered anywhere in the world a pure yellow sweetpea.

Occasionally I was given hints of other secrets of which my mother's mother was made. Once she began to tell me something that she didn't, after all, want me to know. It had happened nearly forty years before, she said. She had done an unimaginably foolish thing — not an immoral, just a ridiculous thing. She started to tell it to me in order to teach me a lesson about my own ego — how I ought not to be so easily and selfishly embarrassed — but suddenly her own ego, that had been forty years before too much like mine, stopped the story. She never gave me that convincing example from her own experience. "Well," she said abruptly, "I'm too humiliated every time I think of it. Just too ashamed. That's a story I'll never tell anybody — not till the day I die."

She died when she was seventy-nine, and nobody ever found out that most carefully kept secret of hers. For every heartbroken person who dies without confessing a great love, there must be at least one proud person who dies without confessing a great humiliation. Perhaps the loves and the humiliations are not so very different from each other; perhaps they are all simply the wounds which prove to us that we are not accidents, that we are unique and that the universe was born with us.

It is not a small thing to take the universe down to the grave with you. I know my mother's mother did not think it was a small thing to die with all those secrets. She would have told us some of them if she could have. She would have left some of her universe behind for us. When she died I understood that I would never know anything about her, and I began to see that probably not until I am dying myself will I be able to believe that so much has died before me.

My father's mother never tried to keep any secrets, and yet I think she must have kept even more than my mother's mother did. She was too humble to think of apologizing for her existence, or to think of requiring anything of me. She wanted only to make me happy, to make me love her. She brought me tiny white bags of lemon drops or wintergreen peppermints and did not expect me to do anything at all but eat them. Maybe she wanted to give me what she had never had.

She had never had candy and she had never had roots and she had never had many smiles. She was orphaned when she was nine and taken from school to do a woman's work. Who took her so she could earn her keep? She was vague about the way she spent those years. "Well, I went to Aunt Clarey's," she would say. "And then Uncle Jake took me over to his place for a spell."

My father's mother never quite understood which of the roots she saw in her tangled world belonged to her. All of the Irish on both sides of my family were obdurate Protestants, but on St. Patrick's Day my father's mother wore green, from her best brilliant satin dress to her bracelet, necklace, and earrings. When I was four years old, she made me a green leprechaun suit and taught me to sing:

O, Paddy dear, and did you hear
The news that's going round?
The shamrock is forbid by law
To grow on Irish ground.
St. Patrick's Day no more we'll keep;
His color can't be seen,
For there's a bloody law ag'in
The wearing o' the green.

When I grew up and found out that orange was the color I ought to be wearing on St. Patrick's Day, I lost a whole history—a whole splendid, martyred, legendary past. I was Irish and yet I wasn't Irish. That symbolic Irish green, green like all the green eyes in our family, did not belong to me after all. It was not I who had taken Napper Tandy by the hand and asked how was poor auld Ireland, and he had never wailed to me that Ireland was the most distressful country I had ever seen, for they were hanging men and women there for wearing of the green.

If I could discover my own roots there, and hers, if I should come around the appropriate grim corner, the loop in time might reveal to me my ancestors selling out to the English and tying the nooses, not swinging from them.

The tangle of my roots (because my grandmothers' roots are mine) became even more bitter in the New World. The father of my mother's mother fought with troops from New York State in the Civil War. He brought back ribbons and medals and certificates and caps and epaulets, all of which were stored in the humpbacked trunk in the spare room of my grandfather's tall prairie house. But the father of my father's mother fought for the South, and his war prizes were not the medals of the victors but the unhealing wounds of the vanquished—the wounds which finally killed him when my grandmother was a tiny girl.

It must have been a little girl like her that James Whitcomb Riley had in mind when he wrote about Little Orphant Annie coming to our house to stay, to wash the cups and saucers up and brush the crumbs away and shoo the chickens off the porch and dust the hearth and sweep and make the fire and bake the bread and earn her board-an'-keep. She did all those things, but at one of the houses where she was earning her board and keep she also learned to play songs and dance tunes on the piano. In all the time I knew her, she was never without a piano, no matter how poor she was, until she moved into a place so small that her piano had to go in order to make room for a davenport that she could make into a bed at night.

When she was fifteen she was given by somebody to a man in a big oval wedding picture, and she went to him to earn her board and keep. John Phillips died long before I was born, and so he never seemed like a grandfather to me; he was only a stone face above a high collar and an odd tie — a face with a wide high brow, wide but narrowed eyes, and a wide thin mouth with a muscular lower lip. It looked as though his teeth were tight against the lip and his tongue was pushed up behind his teeth. Properly several inches below his face is hers. It is surprisingly like the face I have always known, and yet there are so many secrets between that face and the one I first remember, beaming over a small white bag of pink peppermints.

The man in the picture could not have been made entirely of stone. He and my grandmother used to ride horseback fifteen or twenty miles after a full day's work to dance in somebody's barn all night. Then they would ride back in the dawn to another sixteen-hour farm day. The man in the picture never seemed to notice when the girl in the picture began to grow pale. None of her nearly grown family seemed to notice, either. She went on rising at four o'clock in the morning, getting the day's batch of bread ready to bake before anybody else was up, earning her keep. One day they came in from the fields and found her lying unconscious in a pool of what seemed to be all the blood left in her body when she fell.

Then the man with the stone face hitched up the wagon, told the boys to load her in it, and rode off on his horse to fetch the doctor and flag the train.

When the doctor met the wagon somewhere near the end of the twelve-mile trip to town, he said, "She'll never live to get on that train." On the way to Fargo he said, "She'll never live to get to the hospital." While they were unloading her from the ambulance, the Fargo specialist said, "She'll never get to the table, and if she does, she'll never live to get off it." A few hours later he said, "If she makes it through the night, she'll die in the morning. If she lives a week, she'll die at the end of it." That was in 1916, and nobody in North Dakota was using blood transfusions. When my grandmother left the hospital six weeks later, she was whiter than any living human being.

The man with the stone face left her sitting on a chair inside a dimestore window while he ran an errand before taking her to the train. What she always remembered about that half hour in the window was the way all the people passing by stopped to stare at her. They were trying to figure out whether or not she was real. "I just kept a-wishing John would hurry up and take me away from there," she laughed when she told me the story. "I wanted to yell out the window at those people," she said. "I wanted to tell them, 'Don't look at me like that. *I'm* not a *ghost!*' "

If there was a ghost, it was the girl, whoever she was, in the wedding picture. Now that I'm grown, I'm not so sure I am sorry for never having known John Phillips. But when I was small, and had two grandmothers and only one grandfather, I was worried about the balance of things. I wanted to understand about that one grandparent I had never seen — the one who gave me my last name. While I was growing up, I always expected to know, some day, about him and about how things were between the two faces in the oval picture. Now I see that even if John Phillips had lived till I could remember him, the secrets would be as remote as ever.

As remote as they are, the secrets of that world are much closer to me than are the very sights and sounds and smells of it. Still, there is something of those sights and sounds and smells, of those dawn cross-country horseback rides, in my grandmother's hooked rugs.

Once my grandmother laid me down on a starched, ironed gunny sack, drew around me, and made me into a rug. I am three years old; my fingers are spread wide apart, my feet are pointed in opposite directions, and my face is round, with a smile that is almost a complete semicircle. Another of my grandmother's rugs shows herself going to church. She is walking up the steps, with the church behind her, and she wears a green hat and jacket, and holds her purse with her collection money in it.

The same year she made a rug out of me she taught me to sing:

I'll be a sunbeam for Jesus,
To shine for Him each day.
A sunbeam, a sunbeam,
I'll be a sunbeam for Him.

It was always sunny there, in her rug-church world.

When Christmas came in the year of the rug, she dressed me like Santa Claus and sent me into the house where my parents were having a Christmas party. She filled a cloth bag with presents wrapped in different papers so I could tell which gift was meant for which person. I remember how hard it was to hold the bag over my shoulder; my head was too big, my arm too short, my shoulder too small for the classic pose. The bag kept sliding down my arm while she told me how I must behave.

"Now be sure you don't *say* anything! If you say *one word*, they'll know who you are! They'll know you by your voice! But if you don't say a word—just ring your jingle-bells good and loud at the door so they'll let you in, and then hand out your presents, and then *don't say good-by!*—

just ring your bells again — then they'll think *Santa Claus* came!"

I remember all the people who were there: my mother and father, my uncle, my two-month-old baby sister, the Allens and the Dunns. They all laughed in amazement and happiness because Santa Claus had come, and I could hardly keep from laughing myself at the joke I was getting away with. But I never did laugh once; they never got a chance to hear my voice. When I got back to my grandmother, it seemed that we laughed for the rest of the afternoon over the success of her costume and the success of my self-control. Nobody had recognized me.

It was not in my father's mother, as it is not in me, to save money. The only money she ever had was what she earned keeping house for some person who was even much older than she was, but what money she earned always went quickly. She spent it for presents, for clothes, for souvenirs, for pictures taken of her or of me by photographers, for costumes for a lodge dance or a Halloween parade. And all the while she spent her pennies at the Good Will or the Salvation Army or the St. Vincent de Paul or the dime store, my mother's mother was saving.

After she gave up trying to find a yellow sweetpea and left our house, she too became a housekeeper, and finally she worked in an old people's home, where she cooked and made beds till she was seventy-five. To somebody like me, who has never had a savings account, the amount of money she put into postal savings every month was incredible. My mother's mother worried because I whistled, because I laughed too loudly, and because I smiled with my mouth open. My father's mother never seemed to notice how I laughed or whether my teeth were showing when I smiled or whether I kept my legs together when I sat down.

My father's mother always brought me something exciting from the dime store, but it wasn't till I grew up that my mother's mother gave me presents I remember. (Though now I know that for a long time many of the presents under the Christmas tree that were marked "From S.C." were from her Postal Savings account.) When I graduated from high school, she gave me the best suitcase she could find. She herself always traveled with the cheapest cardboard suitcase she could buy at the Rexall drugstore. It is almost as painful to me to use that handsome suitcase as it is to ride my English bicycle and think about her mowing machine wheels.

For Christmas of my freshman year in college she gave me a Bible, perhaps to ease her conscience for giving me the suitcase that took me away, in such style, from the healthful influences on my life. When I was a sophomore she gave me a dictionary, and when I was a junior she gave me Roget's *Thesaurus*. When I was a senior and when I was a graduate student, she "loaned" me the money for my tuition. And every year, my father's mother gave me the prettiest thing she could find in the dime store and a card with a kitten or a bird on it that said, "To a Dear Granddaughter."

Each of them dilutes in me the other. The rectitude of one haunts the gaiety of the other; the prodigality of one subverts the providence of the other. They gave me the gifts of the two hastening clashing cells themselves — the gift of worlds coming together. If I have never successfully reconciled all the gifts, that is hardly their fault. I have been given as much as anybody could decently ask for.

Both of them wanted me to be like them, and each of them thought I was. Neither of them seemed to understand that I could certainly never be made from both of them and still be like either of them.

Both of them wanted to tell me some of their secrets, but neither of them knew how.

And they never stopped coming up with new secrets. My father's mother was nearly seventy years old when she was shopping one day in the dime store and bought herself the smallest box of crayons on the counter. When I came home from school on a weekend visit, she showed me the pictures she had made with them. So far as anybody in the family knew, my grandmother had never drawn a picture before, nor had she ever done anything remotely like drawing a picture. Everybody knew that she could look at a picture in a magazine and, without making a single measurement of herself, cut out a dress that looked, when she had sewed it up and put it on, exactly like the dress in the picture – except, perhaps, for an improvement or two she had seen fit to add. Nobody connected this capacity with the capacity to draw pictures.

She was shy about showing me her pictures because my father had laughed, my uncle had not been interested, and her prospector husband, whom she was about to divorce, had been irate over the money she had thrown away on the crayons.

I was just finishing an art minor, having satisfied myself, and more than satisfied my professors, that whatever else I was going to be, if anything, I was not going to be a potter, an etcher, a lithographer, a sculptor, or a painter in tempera, water color, or oil. The night after I saw what my grandmother could do with eight kindergarten crayons, I cried myself to sleep. But not because I would never be an artist. That was probably the only time I ever cried myself to sleep over somebody else's life.

What might she have told us about herself if anybody had ever listened?

Not so long ago, all the women of my family were together for the last time. It was a summer Sunday afternoon, and the men were gone, as Midwestern men always are after a family dinner. The women, now that the dishes were done, were sitting around the circle of the dinner table, waiting to get up again to help with the Sunday supper. It was the recess between the work of the two meals.

Ever since I was fifteen years old, and a grown woman, the same age as my father's mother on her wedding day, I had had to spend the Sunday afternoon recess at that table. I had to be there because, for some reason I could not quite understand, my relatives, particularly my grandmothers, wanted to *see* me. One of my grandmothers was crocheting and the other was working a puzzle. I sat, as I had sat since I was fifteen, doing nothing. My mother's mother was doing her best to get me involved in her puzzle and I was doing my best to remain uninvolved. It was one of those puzzles that nobody could ever get right. It would say, "Seven down: An old man looks back at his life and finds it – – – –." The first three spaces would have to be "l-o-n." Should the last letter be "e" or "g"? With fifteen or twenty such ambiguities in the puzzle, the owners of the newspaper which published it were fairly safe, according to the laws of probability, in offering bigger prizes every week for the "correct" solution.

My mother, who had majored in mathematics in college, and my father and my husband and I had all tried to make my grandmother see that no matter how many facsimiles of the puzzle she filled in with different variations, she had no chance of winning. But Sunday after Sunday she took on the laws of mathematics. She would buy four or five papers, planning to send in four or five variations. Then she would get carried away by the endless possibilities and trace another twenty or thirty facsimiles, to be sent to the Seattle *Sunday Times* before midnight on Monday.

She was still justifying her existence. She understood the laws of probability as well as anybody, but she believed, as she said, that "a fool has to win now and then, by chance." She hadn't won with the yellow sweetpea, but she was going to win with the Seattle *Times*. An interesting question occurred to me, but I did not ask it. If gambling was an invention of the Devil, which she absolutely believed, then where did one draw the line, in games of chance, between gambling and what she spent all her free Sunday hours doing? Here she was, still trying to make the laws of chance justify her existence when she was nearly seventy-six years old.

If I had been fifteen, and smart enough to think up that question, I would have asked it, but by the time I was smart enough to think up the question, I was thirty-two years old, and I remembered how she had sat for an hour one summer afternoon teaching me to make a terrible noise with a grass blade between my thumbs and then how to whistle like a steam locomotive by blowing into my cupped fists. Or I was remembering how, when we were back on the prairie and she had just fed the chickens and was wearing my grandfather's coveralls and spied, far away on the dusty road, the green car of the Watkins man, she would run for the tall yellow house on the hill, to change into a dress before he arrived. Back there we all dressed for company if we had time. We didn't get much. The Watkins man was, as a matter of fact, very pleasant company.

Now my grandmother, whose eyes could see so far, was looking out, not to the dusty rim of the world, but to the opposite side of our little wet Washington valley. Those hills across from us were as far as anybody could see, even though they were only two miles away. She was looking farther, though — looking east as though she could see the whole long trip she would make three summers later, to sleep beside my grandfather on a North Dakota hillside. That last time she did not travel with a cardboard suitcase.

But I was not thinking then of her next trip east and of the accouterments of it. I could not see that far. I was thinking, as I sat around the circle of the dinner table, of how impatient I was for the recess bell to ring. I was thinking that I had been on display long enough for one day, that I had patiently acknowledged enough advice about myself and my husband and the two great-granddaughters napping in the bedroom. After the advice and the occasional questions about the puzzle, nobody had said anything much to me. They had seen me. And they had talked to each other about the weather, the crops, the relatives back East that I could not remember (unless they were the ones who turned up once a year and lined up in front of their car and passed me from one to another to be kissed), the minister, the minister's sermon that morning, the new highway, the new shopping center.

The night before, my husband and I had been to visit my father's mother. We sat and watched her favorite Westerns on TV. (She was born three years after Custer's Last Stand. I was born two years before the Great Crash of 1929.) On top of her television set was an illuminated sea shell with a Madonna inside it. Beside the shell was a friendship card she had just received from her Secret Pal in the Rebekah Lodge, a painting of Christ personally presented by Oral Roberts, and a ceramic dog she had won at a carnival. The dog would not stand up unless he was propped against the Hollywood Easel Frame which held the picture of Christ.

"Oral Roberts has just been so good to me," my father's mother told us. "He's the preacher on the television, you know. He writes me so many good letters."

The hooked rug of myself hung over the davenport that she would convert into a bed after we were gone. Beside the davenport was a lamp with a sexy ruffled shade over it. The two filaments of the bulb were miraculously shaped into flowers which glowed beneath a tiny statute of Christ on the cross.

After we had watched the Westerns, it was time to go. My grandmother clung to my arm. "Oh, it was so good to *see* you," she said.

But she was looking at me as though she thought that *I* must be the one who could see something. It was like the night my mother took me out when I was a young child to look up into the space over the prairie and count the dots in

Pleiades. If I could see the seventh dot, the papoose on the squaw's back, then according to those people who came before us on the plains, I would grow up to have the keen eyes of the great hunter. My mother was watching my eyes, to see what I could see, and when she knew that I saw, that I surely saw the seventh dot, she was happy, like the mothers of hunters before her, whose children could learn to see far in space.

But I could not see whatever it was that my grandmother wanted me to see, although I think I understood at last what my grandmothers hoped to see when they saw me. During all those years when I looked to them to show me the loop in time, they were looking to me for the same thing. They had been watching me for my secrets, expecting to come around a corner and meet themselves in me. They thought that I must be able to see something they had missed. I had always believed that it was the ones who had gone before me who understood the circle and where they belonged in it, but instead they supposed that it was the ones coming after them who would understand.

We learn one thing from the ones who came before us: how to recognize the dots of our own kind in all the space that is between us. And that recognition is all there can be. As for the secrets—we inherit them with the earth. The hidden is never revealed. Rather, it is the lost secrets of the old people that give the earth its dreadful beauty.

In the end, the first snow falls on the prairie: it is as though the tiny shadow of every star in the sky will fall this once and never again, but the children leaning on their numb elbows worry needlessly; their turn will come long before all of the shadows will pass the windows they are watching. But the children do not really understand this, and they wait, feeling the snow catch at the spinning rim of the wheel they ride, afraid the snow will stop the wheel before they are given their time to play. At last they are set free. They move like dots around the blue circle tramped in the snow. But they are too far apart to see the secrets of each other, the secrets of the circle, the spectres of their own beginnings. And while they are still chasing each other, still shouting to each other through mouths filled with snow, the bell rings and the recess is over.